ACE OF DIAMONDS

ACE of
DIAMONDS

J. MICHAEL BOUCHER

ISBN-13: 9798643761082

Cover and interior design by Stewart A. Williams
Library of Congress Control Number: 2018675309
Printed in the United States of America

DEDICATION

To Marisa, whose unwavering support and insights made this novel possible.

CONVERGING PATHS

ONE

The cracks of three quick .45 caliber pistol shots shattered the nighttime silence. It was a seemingly random act of violence, but the echoes of those shots would soon shatter numerous lives as they reverberated between a small western Pennsylvania town and the Mexican state of Morelos.

Moments earlier, a black 2005 Ford Mustang with only one working headlight had pulled into a seedy strip mall on Grant Street and skidded to a stop on the freshly fallen snow. It did not arrive quietly, as its muffler had long ago rusted through. The three stores in the strip mall that remained in business were closed for the night and secured by metal bars over their windows and doors. Four other storefronts were marked by broken windows, heavy graffiti and faded signs that recalled long-failed businesses.

The Mustang's driver, Cody Timothy Ware, had come to this deserted strip mall because he was desperate. Cody was a pasty-skinned, black-haired twenty-six-year-old who stood five feet, eight inches tall and weighed a meager 135 pounds. He was a heroin addict. Because his body had begun to develop a tolerance for the drug, he needed ever-larger doses to achieve his high. Tonight, he sought "Ace of Diamonds," a powerful new brand of street heroin that had already inflicted several fatal overdoses. Perversely, what attracted Cody was the very fact that "Ace" was powerful enough to kill.

Cody was no stranger to the drug scene, and he expected tonight to be just another routine buy. On a rare visit to his parent's home earlier in the week, he had stolen some of his mother's jewelry and pawned it. He was flush with cash. Cody took a long drag from his cigarette, exhaled slowly and muttered to his girlfriend, "OK, Brandi, let's get this done. We're out of dope, and we could be snowed in tomorrow."

Brandi, a vacant-eyed 25-year-old bleached blond, didn't respond. She just stared into the darkness, seeing nothing but swirling snow illuminated by the one functioning streetlight at the far end of the parking lot. She absentmindedly stroked the blond hair of her three-year old daughter, who was sitting on her lap. At least tonight she felt relatively safe, which for her was an unfamiliar feeling. For the last several years she had been living with an abusive and volatile man. Several weeks earlier, after a particularly violent argument with her boyfriend over dirty dishes in the kitchen sink that left her with a black eye and two missing teeth, Brandi had taken their daughter and moved to a cheap one-room apartment above a consignment store. A few days later she met Cody who, having no place else to go and some drugs to share, moved in with her that evening.

Brandi suddenly tensed, sensing some unseen but ominous danger. She checked to see that the door was locked and pulled her daughter closer. In a panicked voice she said,

"Cody, I've got a really bad feeling about this. I'm scared, let's get the hell out of here!"

"Don't worry babe, I know what I'm doing. We'll be outta here in two minutes. I don't know about you, but I'm getting dope sick. I can't make it through the night if we don't score."

Cody smiled with anticipation as a solitary figure stepped out of the darkness and headed for his side of the Mustang. This wasn't his first rodeo. Although the pusher's identity was obscured by the swirling snow and dim light, Cody was unconcerned because he had received a text earlier in the day telling him where and when to meet.

Surprising Cody, the man suddenly diverted to the passenger side. Cody slammed his fist on the steering wheel and yelled, "What the fuck is he doing? Here, Brandi, take the cash and tell him that we want a bun of Ace." Brandi hesitated, then slowly began to roll down the window. She found herself facing a large man with a pistol aimed at her head. Brandi shrieked, and then her world went dark as a .45 caliber round struck her above her right eye, leaving an exit wound the size of a grapefruit on the back of her skull and splattering blood and brain tissue over the car and its two other occupants. The next two rounds struck Cody in his right shoulder and right temple. Cody slumped forward against the steering wheel, his head landing on the horn and causing it to blare incessantly.

The dealer spat on the ground, then calmly turned and walked to the secluded spot where he had left his pickup truck.

TWO

Franklin Police Department
11 P.M.

Officer Matt Riley hated the midnight shift. He had spent most of his twenty-six years in Franklin, and had a good idea of what happened there after dark. If he was lucky, tonight's shift would be a couple of DUI arrests and maybe a domestic disturbance call. He would not be lucky.

If you weren't born here you sure as hell wouldn't move here, Matt thought. After graduating from high school, he had tried to escape Franklin by joining the Marine Corps. An athletic, muscular man standing six foot three and weighing 215 pounds, Matt thought that he had found a home in the Marines. That dream died one morning on the bank of a canal in Helmand province, Afghanistan, when he was seriously wounded by a Taliban machine gun burst. He was medically discharged from the Marines and returned to Franklin. After a long and painful recovery, Matt signed on with the Franklin police department.

Despite his heavy uniform jacket, Matt shivered as he walked out of the station to his patrol car. The gusting winds made the actual temperature of five degrees feel like 10 below zero, and snow was beginning to blanket the town. Matt thought that the weather alone should be enough to keep any reasonable person off the streets, but he knew that some Franklin residents fell far outside any definition of "reasonable."

Matt brushed the snow from his coat and jumped into his cruiser and its promise of warmth. He turned the key and the engine seemed to protest as it slowly cranked and reluctantly started. While the car warmed up, Matt grabbed an ice scraper from the floor and stepped back into the blowing snow to clear the windshield. "Shit," he muttered as he stepped on a patch of ice and just barely maintained his balance by steadying himself on the fender.

After clearing the windshield, Matt hopped back inside and headed out on patrol. As he looked around, he was struck by how the once prosperous town was struggling. Several blocks of the main thoroughfare, Liberty Street, still reminded him of a picture postcard of a prosperous 1950s city, with charming brick buildings and neatly trimmed parks. Beyond that, once-stately homes had gradually fallen into varying states of disrepair as an aging population with diminishing incomes struggled to make ends meet. As the older generation died off, it seemed that much of the town was dying with it. Further away, areas such as Third Ward were marked by ramshackle homes, some on the verge of being condemned, inhabited by a diffident younger generation that itself seemed to be on the verge of condemnation.

As he turned onto Liberty Street, he was startled when the police radio crackled, "Unit 7, Code 415 at the Grant Street mall. Anonymous caller, gunshots fired – no further details."

His senses now on full alert, Matt picked up his microphone and responded, "10-4, Unit 7 rolling." Matt gunned the engine and headed towards Third Ward.

THREE

Grant Street
11:20 P.M.

Matt pulled into the strip mall parking lot, not knowing what to expect. A black Mustang was parked at the far end of the otherwise deserted parking lot, and his headlights illuminated exhaust fumes curling from its tailpipe. As he pulled closer, he could hear the Mustang's horn blaring. *What the hell is going on here?*

Matt shined his spotlight on the Mustang, and a chill ran down his spine. He saw a shattered driver's side window, and there was a body slumped forward against the steering wheel. A closer look revealed something splattered on the inside of the windshield.

Matt's voice betrayed his stress. "Unit 7, officer in need of assistance at the strip mall on Grant. Looks like I've got two gunshot victims here. I need an ambulance."

"10-4, Unit 7. Backup and an ambulance are on the way. Do you have an active shooter?"

"Negative. At least I don't see anyone, but I just got here."

Matt carefully scanned the area to confirm that the shooter was gone, and then focused on the carnage in the Mustang. Suddenly and involuntarily, his mind transported him back to Afghanistan. He was engulfed by the sounds and the smells of battle. In his mind's eye he could see himself dragging a wounded comrade, with rounds snapping past their heads and dirt and rock shards stinging his skin as he slowly crawled towards safety. Then, with a sickening splat, the man's head exploded into a formless lump of bloody flesh. At that point, as it always did, the flashback ended.

Matt felt a rage boiling inside him and slammed his fist against the steering wheel. "Goddammit, No!" After a minute, he regained control and mumbled to himself, "It don't mean nothin." That was their mantra when a buddy got blown away. As if it could make the fear and the pain and the inhumanity vanish. "It don't mean nothin."

Matt composed himself, got out of the car, pistol drawn, and found a spot where he had some cover but could observe the Mustang. There were no other signs of life in the parking lot. Other than those he had made, there were no tire tracks or footprints in the snow. Matt judged that, given the rate that the snow was falling, whatever went down here must have happened at least 15 minutes ago.

The sound of an approaching siren melded with the blaring of the horn, and the flashing lights of another police cruiser entering the parking lot set off an eerie, multicolored light show in the falling snow. Lieutenant Ray Tucker erupted from the cruiser with gun drawn. He motioned to Matt to approach the driver's side while he stationed himself at the right rear of the car in a shooting stance. "Son of a bitch, Matt I can hear a baby crying in there!"

Matt shined his flashlight into the car. "Holy mother of God, I see it. It's covered with blood, and lying on the floorboard on the passenger side. There's a woman on the passenger side unconscious with a bad head wound." Matt holstered his pistol, then opened the car door and pulled the driver back against the seat, stopping the horn. "The driver is a white male with what looks like multiple gunshot wounds. I've got a pulse, but he's unresponsive."

In the dim light, Matt could see that the driver was bleeding heavily. His experience told him that what looked like a huge quantity of blood might not be serious, and he began applying pressure to the head wound to stop the bleeding just as the Venango County EMS truck arrived. The paramedic called out to Lieutenant Tucker, "Ray, are we secure?" She had learned the hard way to be sure that there was not an active shooter before assisting at a crime scene.

"Yeah, Rhoda Mae, we're secure. We've got three victims, so you better get to work."

Rhoda Mae walked to the Mustang and opened the passenger door. She'd seen a lot during her fifteen years as a paramedic, and quickly sized up the situation. "You've got a female with a gunshot wound to the head. Half her skull is gone, she never had a chance. No respiration, no pulse, brain matter blown all over the car and she's bled out." She glanced at her watch and said, "I'm pronouncing her at 11:35."

Next, she carefully lifted the crying child out of the car and examined her. "Looks like about a three- or four-year old girl, covered in blood, but I think it's the passenger's blood. I can't see any obvious injuries, but I won't know for sure until I get a better look." Rhoda Mae handed the baby to the driver, "Put her in the back of the truck and wrap her in a blanket. I'll be right there." She moved to the driver's side and leaned in front of Matt. "Give me some more light so that I see what we've got here. I've got a good pulse. Airway is clear and he's breathing OK. Man, he's one lucky son of a bitch - if that head wound was a little further to the left he'd be gone."

Matt looked a little closer at the driver and said, "Aw, crap. I know this guy. I went to high school with him."

The EMS driver had already unloaded the gurney and wheeled it to the driver's side. Matt and the paramedic grunted as they lifted the bloody body from the driver's seat and placed it on the gurney. "Ok, let's get him in the truck." As she jumped in with her patient, Rhoda Mae shouted to the driver, "UPMC Northwest."

As the EMS vehicle sped away, its flashing lights and siren gradually disappearing into the distance, Lieutenant Tucker shined his flashlight into the Mustang. On the console between the front seats he saw a wallet coated with blood and brain tissue, and in the dead passenger's hand a roll of bills. "Interesting, there's a roll of bills still here; whatever the hell happened it wasn't a robbery." Reluctantly, he picked up the wallet. *Pennsylvania license, he's a local but I don't recognize him.*

"The male victim is Cody Ware, 1340 Eagle Street. Is that your guy?"

"Yes, sir. Like I said, we went to high school together, but I haven't seen him since. You know what that area of town is like, and I guess that tells us something about him. Most of the places over there are real shitholes."

"I better wake up the Chief - he won't want to wait until the morning to hear about this one. I'll call in the coroner. You head over to the ER and see what you can sort out."

"I'm on it."

FOUR

Augustine's Ristorante, Pittsburgh
Monday, December 18
12:15 A.M.

In barely an hour, news of the Franklin shooting had already reached Gus Amoroso in Pittsburgh. He was angry, and there would be serious consequences.

Gus Amoroso was a study in contrasts. He had been born to an Italian father and a Mexican mother, and each left their imprint on him. As a teenager, Gus had cut his teeth in his mother's family business, which had its roots in the Mexican state of Morelos and controlled a substantial portion of the Pittsburgh heroin trade. While his family connections got him into the business, it was his cunning and vicious streak, coupled with the mysterious disappearance of his two principal rivals, that led to his uncontested control of that business by the time he was thirty-five. Yet, Gus also acquired a refined side from his father, the proprietor of Augustine's Ristorante, one of the leading Italian restaurants in the Northeastern United States.

To all appearances, Gus was a reputable and wealthy businessman. In his father's mold, he wore finely tailored clothes and considered himself – with good reason – to be a connoisseur of

Italian food and fine wines. Several restaurant critics had observed that, but for its off-the-beaten-path Pittsburgh location, Augustine's merited two Michelin stars. Gus spent much of his time at the restaurant because it concealed his criminal empire within a legitimate business, allowing him to meet with his business associates without raising any suspicions.

Although Augustine's was not open for business at this late hour, Gus was sitting at his desk in the plush private office that he maintained on the second floor. He calmly poured some Vin Santo, swirled the caramel colored dessert wine in his glass and contemplated the discussion he was about to have. As he did so, he unconsciously but methodically broke each of the five pencils that had been sitting in a cup on his desk. *What the hell was Tony thinking? Now I have to clean up his mess before it affects my business. And send a message that people need to listen to me very carefully in the future.*

The message that he intended to send was of no small importance. Gus' drug empire covered Pennsylvania and much of the Midwest. All told, he employed more than 350 people, ranging from mid-level dealers responsible for specific geographic areas, such as Tony in Franklin, to low-level employees who cut and packaged drugs and had no clue that they were a part of his organization. Given the nature of their work, they tended to be violent and not easily controlled. The message that Gus intended to send was that failure to follow his rules would not be tolerated.

A soft knock on the door intruded on his thoughts.

"Come in. The door's unlocked."

Tony entered the office. "You wanted to see me, Mr. Amoroso?"

Gus spoke calmly, but there was a subtle menace in his voice. "Yes, thank you for coming so quickly. I've heard some disturbing news from Franklin, and I want to hear your version of what happened before I act."

Tony knew that the absence of an invitation to sit down, along with the coldness in Gus' voice, was a bad sign. "Mr. Amoroso, I'm sorry - it was a screw up. One of my guys flaked out. Myron Foley – everyone calls him MF?" He paused to see if Gus knew who he meant and got a dismissive shrug that meant either that he didn't know or didn't care. "Well, MF was selling in Third Ward. Turns out that his ex-girlfriend showed up with a new boyfriend and MF's daughter." Tony tried but couldn't keep from laughing. "Who could have seen that one coming? Anyway, MF drilled her with a .45 round. Popped the boyfriend a couple times too."

You hire a guy called MF and you're surprised when he pops someone? Gus locked eyes with Tony and paused to calm himself as well as to consider his words before he spoke. "Tony, you've let me down. I gave you a position of responsibility because I thought that you could handle it. But now I learn your people are out of control. I won't allow that, Tony."

Gus continued, "You know that business has been very good for us. That's because we have understandings with certain people in Franklin that took years to develop. All of that will fall apart if we attract attention to ourselves."

Tony started to respond but Gus silenced him with a murderous glare. "We have to clean up your mess quickly. With a shooting that everyone knows is drug-related, the press and the police will be all over it. I try very hard not to come to the attention of the authorities. Your friend MF has become a liability that must be addressed. Do we understand each other?"

"Sure, Mr. Amoroso, let me give this some thought and I'll let you know what I come up with."

"No, Tony, I don't want to hear your plans. This is not rocket science. I think you know what has to be done. If you can't fix this problem quickly, then you are no longer of any use to me. All I want to hear is that the problem is fixed."

As Tony turned to leave the office, Gus said, "Take my driver with you when you go to Franklin. He can be very helpful."

FIVE

UPMC Emergency Room, Seneca
12:30 A.M.

A tall woman, with sharp features and short brown hair that was just beginning to gray, walked into the ER waiting room. She was a physician, and she exuded a sense of confidence and control over her domain. She scanned the room, seeing mostly tired and disheveled people of the sort that frequent ERs in the early morning hours, and then noticed a police officer standing against a far wall.

Ignoring several impatient people trying to attract her attention, she walked towards Matt. As she approached, Matt quickly sized her up, guessing her age to be about 40 and noting approvingly that she obviously found time in her schedule to keep in shape. "Officer, I'm Dr. Sally Bridges. Are you here about the gunshot victim?"

"Yeah, him and the little girl that they brought in at the same time. How are they doing?"

In a tired, emotionless voice, Dr. Bridges replied, "The head wound looked a lot worse than it was. Basically, the bullet creased his skull and took a chunk out of his ear. He's going to have a hell of a headache. The shoulder wound is superficial. We're going to admit him for a day or so just to make sure that there are no complications, but I don't expect any problems."

"And the little girl?"

Dr. Bridges sighed. "She wasn't injured tonight, but there are signs of previous abuse. She had a couple of old fractures that seemed to have healed up pretty well, and a suspicious burn on her arm. She's also suffered serious emotional trauma tonight. Her mother is the woman who was shot to death in the car. Mr. Ware says that he's not the father, so we've called Child Protective Services."

"What a mess. Well, let's start with we've got a warrant for Ware on a prior drug charge, and we haven't sorted out what went down tonight. So, he's under arrest. When can I talk with him?"

"He's awake now. We only used a local on him. I can't give him any painkillers until the labs come back - no telling what else is in his system - so he's going to be uncomfortable."

"OK. Any reason I can't handcuff him to the bed?"

Dr. Bridges bristled at that notion. "Is that really necessary? This is a hospital, not a jail. And I seriously doubt that he's going anywhere in his condition."

"You might be surprised. Unless you tell me that there is some overriding medical reason, yes it's necessary."

Dr. Bridges gave Matt a cold look. "No, there's no medical reason not to. Come with me." She turned and pushed her way through a door with a large red "No Admittance" sign and walked briskly down a tiled corridor. Matt's nose wrinkled at the antiseptic smells of the ER. Stopping at the third cubicle on the left, she pulled back the curtain and said to Matt, "he'll be in here until we can admit him."

"OK. We'll have an officer guarding him until he's released for transport to the jail. Since no one else is available, I guess that for now I'm the lucky one."

"Suit yourself, just stay out of the way. We have a lot going on tonight. If you insist on handcuffing him, use his left arm, and be careful not to pull the IV line that's running across his chest. I'll send the nurse in to make sure everything is OK. Now, if you'll excuse me, I have patients to see."

"Thanks," Matt said to her back as she walked down the corridor. He looked into the cubicle and studied his prisoner. Cody was lying on the hospital bed, with bandages covering the top of his head and his right shoulder. His eyes had a vacant stare, and although he looked towards the door he focused on nothing in particular. *How did this guy get so screwed up? You've got a warrant out for your arrest, someone just tried to blow your head off, and we still haven't solved the mystery of the woman lying on a slab in the morgue and the little girl that you brought along with you for a drug buy. Way to go, sport. If they gave medals for all around fuck ups, you'd get the gold.*

Matt approached the side of the bed and carefully snapped his handcuffs around Cody's wrist and attached the other to the bed frame. "Cody, how are you? Do you know who I am?" Cody's only response was to turn toward the wall and close his eyes.

"I hate to do this, man, but I'm placing you under arrest. You've got an outstanding warrant, and there may be additional charges based on what happened tonight. Do you understand me?"

Cody mumbled, "I hear you."

"I found you in a car tonight along with a woman and a

small child, and I'd like to ask you some questions about that. Are you willing to talk with me?"

"How is Brandi?"

"Is that the woman who was with you?"

"Yes."

"Before we talk, Cody, I need to read you your *Miranda* rights."

"Don't waste your time, I know all that crap." Cody started to recite the words that he had heard on numerous TV cop dramas, but Matt stopped him.

"It doesn't work that way, Cody, I have to do this by the book." In a formal tone, Matt began the recitation, "Mr. Ware, you have the right to remain silent. . ."

Cody acknowledged that he understood his rights and asked, "So how is Brandi?"

"I'm sorry to have to tell you that she passed away."

Cody's body went rigid and his face paled. For a moment he was obviously gathering his thoughts, and looked to be on the verge of tears. Then the color returned to his face and his look hardened. "I thought it would be OK. What the fuck happened?"

"I'm going to need you to help me figure that out. Are you willing to waive your right to an attorney?"

"Sure, why not? Now tell me what happened."

Matt was taken aback by how quickly Cody's sense of vulnerability had shifted to a cold, defiant attitude. "What we know is that she was shot in the face at close range with a large caliber handgun. She died instantly. What we don't know is who did it, and why. And we don't know who the little girl is."

Cody paused again, and responded in a soft, unsure voice. "Daisy. Her name is Daisy." His voice cracked as he asked, "Is she dead too?"

"No. She wasn't injured tonight." *Although it looks like someone has been abusing her pretty badly. I wonder if that's how you get your kicks. We'll get to that later.* "Her last name?"

"I don't know. Brandi just called her Daisy."

"And Brandi's last name?"

"Jennings."

"It would help a lot if you could tell me what happened in that parking lot."

"Dude came up to the passenger window - that was weird. He started out heading to the driver's side, and then suddenly veered to the passenger side. Then Brandi screamed and there was a big yellow flash. Next thing I knew I was in the ambulance."

"You were there for a drug buy?"

Cody suddenly realized that he was on very dangerous ground. "No, you asshole, I was doing some last-minute Christmas shopping. I'm done talking. I want a lawyer."

"OK. So be it. But let me say a few things to you as a friend, and you don't need to answer me. I'm wondering why the hell you're laying here in a hospital bed with a bullet hole in your head. And I can't even begin to imagine why you had that little girl with you."

Cody started to speak, but Matt put his hand out in a command to remain quiet until he finished what he had to say.

"When I was in the Corps, I saw some pretty good people get fucked up on drugs. A few of them were good friends.

They all thought they had it under control. I think some of them needed the stuff just to cope with the shit that we saw in Afghanistan." Matt realized that he was getting tense and his voice was rising. He paused and took a deep breath before continuing, "They didn't have it under control. It was controlling them. Before long, most of those guys ended up in the brig or in a body bag."

Matt leaned forward, stared into Cody's eyes and spoke with a slow, firm voice, "I don't need to wait for the tox report to come back to know that you're high on something right now. You're going down a bad road, Cody, and you need to get some help."

Matt stepped back from the bed. "So you go get your lawyer, and you better find a good one. Because, when we sort this mess out, you're going to be looking at some serious charges. If nothing else, you're going to be facing a child endangerment charge for bringing that little girl on a drug buy. And believe me, you're not going to get any sympathy from any judge or jury on that one."

Slowly, Cody raised his right arm as far as the IV would permit and extended his middle finger.

"I'll be outside. Think about it, Cody."

SECTION II
DEGREES OF POWER

ONE

Walter Kelliher was in a foul mood. A diminutive, rapidly balding thirty-five year old whose face still showed signs of severe childhood acne, he sat fidgeting behind a large, highly polished mahogany desk. He was dressed in a pinstriped Brooks Brothers suit, button-down blue shirt and a maroon tie. Kelliher pulled his thick, black-framed glasses from his face and rubbed his nose as he fumed over the implications of last night's shooting.

Kelliher had been Franklin's Mayor for three years, and very much wanted to keep that job in next year's election. Previously, he had been an unimpressive salesman at the local Ford dealership, the sort of person who people mocked and avoided. As Mayor, however, he considered himself someone to be reckoned with. Yet, he was painfully aware that his election had been a fluke, the result of the popular incumbent being indicted for federal tax fraud and withdrawing from the race one week before the election.

His reelection prospects were crumbling as the local economy continued on a death spiral. Franklin once had been a prosperous city, its economy fueled by the enormous wealth that flowed into the region beginning in the 1860s, with the discovery of oil in nearby Titusville. By the 1990s, oil companies such as Pennzoil and Quaker State had moved their headquarters – and their jobs – to Texas. All that they left behind was the faded glory of once imposing buildings and the shattered dreams of the newly unemployed. In the following decades, Franklin's remaining large employers, unable to compete in a global economy, began to fail or move offshore.

The challenges facing Franklin were not Kelliher's fault, but he was ill-suited by education or experience to address them. Instead, he tried to shift blame to others, and he was focused on that strategy when the sound of knuckles sharply rapping on his door intruded. Kelliher looked up and then snarled, "Get your ass in here, Chief."

Chief Robert Miller was an imposing, barrel-chested man of moderate height who wore his salt-and-pepper hair close cropped, and who found some element of humor in all but the most serious situations. He entered Kelliher's office, gave him a hard look, and without waiting for an invitation sat down. In a booming bass voice, Miller asked, "What's on your mind, Mayor?"

Kelliher was offended by Miller's attitude, and in his high-pitched, nasally voice demanded, "Just what the hell happened last night at the Grant Street mall? I have a press conference in fifteen minutes, and that will come up."

"We're still investigating. What we know at this point is that a 25-year-old female was killed by a gunshot to the head, and her three-year old daughter was unharmed but traumatized. The driver of the car, a 26-year-old male, was shot a couple of times but wasn't seriously injured. He should be out of the hospital in a day or two. He's not talking, and he's already hired Elliot Z. Finkleman, Esquire." Chief Miller practically spat out the lawyer's name with a contemptuous tone.

"I thought that bastard had his law license suspended?"

"It was. He got caught taking marijuana from a client in lieu of his usual fee. But he completed his rehab, and the bar reinstated his license last month."

"Who was the shooter?" Kelliher demanded. "And why did this happen?"

"We have no idea who the shooter was, or why he popped them. But it doesn't take a genius to figure out that drugs were involved."

Kelliher, worried that his reelection prospects would be harmed by a drug-related murder, snarled at Miller. "You don't know who did it, or why, but yet you claim it's drug related? I'm not buying it. I have enough on my plate without you spreading unfounded rumors that we've had another drug-related murder here in Franklin. So what I want to hear is that it was just another domestic dispute."

Chief Miller looked at Kelliher incredulously, "Who the hell do you think you're fooling, Mayor? Everyone over the age of ten knows that there's a serious drug problem here, and it's getting worse each year. That area on Grant Street where the shooting occurred – in fact, most of Third Ward – is a known turf for heroin dealers. We're not immune to the opioid crisis, Mayor. Hell, last year we had almost 3,000 drug-related deaths in the state, and at least ten here in Venango County."

"Chief, try speaking English. What the hell is an opioid?"

Miller slowly shook his head and looked at Kelliher in disbelief as he said, "You can't pick up a newspaper or watch the TV news without seeing something on the opioid crisis." Miller sighed heavily and continued. "Well, I guess the first step is to try to help you understand what we're facing on the streets."

Kelliher responded testily, "I don't need you to tell me what's going on in my town, Miller, and I don't appreciate your attitude."

Miller ignored the rebuke and continued. "It's really pretty simple. Opioids are a type of narcotic that includes prescription drugs, like oxycodone and morphine, and a whole bunch of really bad illegal stuff like heroin and fentanyl. The heroin is coming in from Mexico, and gangs in Pittsburgh and Detroit distribute it here. You ought to sit down with one of the local docs to get the complete picture, but I can tell you this – street heroin is a hell of a lot stronger than the prescription painkillers, and all that crap is really addictive. What really scares me is fentanyl – it's fifty times more potent than heroin."

Miller paused to see if the Mayor was following him, and then continued, "All of my officers, and the EMS responders, now carry Narcan." He saw Kelliher's confused look and added, "It's an antidote that can reverse an opioid overdose. Last month one of my officers was exposed to fentanyl during a traffic stop and it caused him to OD. If his supervisor hadn't responded and administered the Narcan, he'd be dead. Hell, we even have Narcan kits in our high school. Think about that, Mayor. It used to be that school nurses couldn't even hand out an aspirin, and now they have Narcan in case one of their teenage students overdoses."

Kelliher pounded the table and screamed, "I really don't give a damn, Chief, and I sure as hell don't need a lecture from you. If some losers want to take this shit and kill themselves, that's their problem. Hell, we'd probably all be better off to get rid of them – that'd thin out the shallow end of the gene pool. Now listen very carefully to me: this murder is *not* a drug deal gone bad. We do *not* have a drug problem here in Franklin. When you do your job and investigate it, I'm sure that it *will* turn out to be some sort of a domestic dispute, won't it?"

"Mayor, you're dead wrong. We can't ignore the drug problem or a lot of otherwise good people are going to die. Heroin is cheaper and easier to get than beer, even for junior high school kids. We can't arrest our way out of the problem because as fast as we can bust the dealers, new ones take their places. If I bust an addict, he spends maybe 20 to 30 days in jail, and as soon as he gets out, he goes back to using."

Mayor Kelliher had turned red in the face and snarled, "Chief, I'm tired of your bleeding heart bullshit, so spare me the sermon. I want the shooter in custody in 48 hours, and I don't want there to be drug charges - it's a simple homicide. If you can't handle that I'll find someone who can to take your place. Now get out of my office."

Chief Miller's face darkened, and he rose from his chair and leaned forward so that his face was six inches from Kelliher's. His voice took on a menacing tone as he said, "Mayor, you can have my resignation any time you'd like it, so don't waste your breath trying to threaten me. The fact is, I'm not exactly thrilled working for a failed car salesman with delusions of grandeur who won't be sitting behind that desk next year. And don't waste your time trying to act like you're some sort of tough guy. Because, trust me, you're not."

Chief Miller straightened and glared down at Kelliher. "Now, I've got work to do." The Chief turned and walked out the door.

TWO

Juan Sanchez-Torres, better known as "El Animal," was deeply anxious, as only someone whose life hangs in the balance can be. He was dressed casually, sipping Espolòn tequila while sitting on an elegantly landscaped terrace overlooking an enormous infinity pool behind his mansion in Cuernavaca, a city of about 350,000 people in the South Central Mexican state of Morelos. El Animal, a muscular, black-haired man of average height who wore an unkempt black moustache, was the number two man in the Grupos de Morelos ("GDM") drug cartel. This morning he had initiated a plan to assassinate the current leader and become the undisputed head of the GDM. If his plan failed, he would die before sunset.

El Animal, as he became known after committing a series of vicious murders to reinforce his position within the GDM, usually felt safe in his home. Cuernavaca was a weekend retreat for many wealthy residents of Mexico City, about ninety minutes away by car, and not typically affected by drug violence. Few in the drug trade would be so foolish as to challenge El Animal. Not one to leave anything to chance,

31

however, El Animal had installed the latest high tech security features in his home, and maintained a well-trained and heavily armed guard force around the clock. Today, however, a Beretta 9 mm pistol sat on the table in front of him. The weapon was not for self-defense; if his plan failed he would use it to take his own life rather than face torture for a failed assassination attempt.

As he sipped his tequila, 100 kilometers away a small force of highly trained former Cuerpo de Fuerzas Especiales (Mexican Special Forces) soldiers, loyal only to El Animal, was setting an ambush. Its mission was to assassinate Hector Carillo, the GDM leader, as he drove along an isolated stretch of road leading to one of the key GDM operations in the neighboring state of Guerrero. El Animal had carefully planned the ambush over a three-month period, and this morning he learned that Carillo would be traveling through the planned ambush zone accompanied by only a small security detail.

If his plan succeeded, it would appear that the rival Los Zetas cartel had assassinated Carillo in one of a seemingly endless series of inter-cartel battles. For that to happen, El Animal's forces would have to quickly kill Carillo and his entire security force, escape undetected and leave subtle signs that the assassination was the handiwork of the rival cartel. If Carillo or any of his security detail survived, or if there were any unexpected witnesses, El Animal's treachery would be revealed and anyone associated with him would die painfully.

El Animal's motivations were quite simple: greed and lust for power. The GDM had a very profitable business producing Mexican white heroin and exporting it into the United

States, and the profits from that business provided immense wealth and power to its leaders. Through bribery and, where necessary, violence, the GDM controlled many important government and police officials. El Animal's share of the GDM profits would have made him a billionaire, had he not squandered most of his money on a lavish lifestyle. Ironically, although El Animal refused to use heroin, lest he become addicted, he had become addicted to a different high – the wealth and power that flowed from the heroin trade. He was willing to risk all to maintain that particular high.

Viewed dispassionately, the GDM was a sophisticated international business operation that engaged in the production, importation across the southwestern US border and distribution of a vast quantity of a highly popular powder-like product. As a sideline, its financial arm engaged in large-scale money laundering. A senior GDM 'executive' was responsible for each of these functions, and had several mid-level 'executives' reporting to him. All of the GDM activities were carefully compartmentalized, such that employees knew only about their particular function. Anyone who became unduly curious about other GDM activities would quickly be "outplaced."

The GDM had a particularly strong retail distribution network in the American East and Midwest regions. El Animal had installed loyal relatives in key leadership positions. He took pride in the fact that he had increased the efficiency and sales volume of the organization, much as would an American MBA responsible for selling a different white power - laundry detergent. The difference was that what El Animal lacked in high-powered business skills – his formal education having ended in the third grade – he made up for with a native cunning. El Animal also had the advantage of looser HR guidelines than those followed by a corporation. If an employee screwed up, or in some other way displeased El Animal, his employment would be terminated by means of a bullet to the back of the head.

El Animal was distracted from his worries over whether the assassination attempt would succeed by the sight of his girlfriend pulling herself out of the pool. Rema was a stunning blond American girl of about eighteen. One of her more charming habits, El Animal thought, was that when she was in the mood for a swim she simply shed all of her clothes and dove in. Rema was nearly six feet tall, with a perfectly tanned and superbly toned body. El Animal was not naïve enough to think that she was attracted to him for his looks; no, this girl was attracted to wealth and power. As she walked toward him he became aroused at the sight of the water dripping from her breasts and running down her body. Sensing that he was watching her, Rema adopted an exaggerated gait that caused her breasts to bounce delightfully as her hips swayed suggestively. She paused briefly just out of his reach and with her back to him bent over to pick up her towel, which caused El Animal to drop his drink. As she toweled off and then nestled into his lap, she had his complete and undivided attention.

El Animal lifted her from the chair and laid her on the adjoining lounge. He was beginning to remove his pants when he heard his bodyguard cough loudly to get his attention and whisper, from a discrete distance, "Jefe, I'm sorry to interrupt, but Senor Cardenas is here. You told me to interrupt you no matter what you were doing when he arrived."

As Rema covered herself with a towel and looked on

with amusement, the guard stood terrified waiting to see whether El Animal's legendary volcanic temper would erupt. The guard knew that he would be punished severely if he disobeyed his instructions to let El Animal know immediately when Cardenas arrived, but feared that interrupting him when he was about to fuck his girlfriend was a no-win situation.

El Animal looked at the guard and snarled, "Is he alone?"

The guard nodded and said, "Si."

"Show him to the game room and tell him I will be there in a minute." El Animal turned to the girl and said, "I must speak to this man, cariño, but I'll be back in five minutes."

El Animal retrieved the pistol from the table, tucked it into the waistband behind his back, and walked into the house. As he entered the game room, he could sense from the relaxed demeanor of Arturo Cardenas that the ambush had succeeded. The man stood and faced him.

"Congratulations, El Jefe. Things could not have gone better. Carillo is dead, as are all of his guards. There are no witnesses, and when the policía federale comes across the dead bodies they will conclude from all of the evidence that we left that this was the act of Los Zetas."

El Animal broke into a broad grin, "How long will it be before the bodies are discovered?"

"We have arranged for someone to 'accidentally' discover them and anonymously report to the authorities tomorrow morning."

"Excellent. When the others learn that Carillo is dead, I will finalize my control. You have done well, Arturo, and you will be rewarded. Thank you for coming, but if you will excuse me, I have much work to do to consolidate my control. I will be in touch."

"Thank you, Jefe." Cardenas turned and left the game room.

El Animal pulled his smart phone from his pocket and tapped an icon on its screen that opened an app that enabled encrypted voice phone calls. *Amazing how these foolish Americans make it so easy for us to break their laws. I can talk with my colleagues in complete privacy, and leave no record of my calls.* He scrolled down his directory, found the name that he was looking for and tapped it. Two thousand miles and two time zones away, Gus Amoroso heard the peculiar tone that told him that he had an incoming encrypted call, pulled the phone from his pocket and answered.

"Buenas tardes, Juan." Gus was one of the few people who dared call El Animal by his given name.

"Hola, Gus. Are you alone?"

"Si."

El Animal chuckled and said, "I have some interesting news to share with you, mi primo. It seems that there has been an unfortunate event here earlier today that I thought might interest you. Senior Carillo was ambushed a couple of hours ago, and sadly, Carillo and everyone who was with him seems to have died. Because it was on an isolated road in Morelos, there were no witnesses. I thought you might want to light a candle at church in his memory or something."

"Yes, Juan, that is very interesting and very sad. I will surely light a candle for our late, lamented leader. And who is suspected of committing this horrible act?"

"Also very interesting, Gus, when the policía discover the

murders tomorrow they will conclude that is was done by Los Zetas. This will be a very difficult time, as the GDM naturally will want vengeance."

With a mock serious tone, Gus responded, "Ah yes, there will be a demand for vengeance. It will take a strong leader to keep the GDM focused on business and not waste its resources on fighting the Zetas. I wonder who that new leader will be – anyone that I know, Juan?"

"Ah, funny that you should ask, Gus, but I believe that my colleagues will expect me to take Carillo's place at this difficult time. Despite the enormous sacrifice that it would involve, I believe it is my duty to accept." El Animal's voice changed from lightly sarcastic to a serious tone. "Let's be serious for a minute. The plan that you helped me develop has succeeded, and I will now control the GDM. I need you down here for a couple of weeks to help me consolidate power and implement our strategic plans. When can you get here?"

Gus thought for a moment and said, "I have a minor problem that I need to address here, it should not take too long, and then I will join you, cousin."

"The sooner the better, Gus. We have much work to do. Call me when you've made your arrangements."

"Of course. Adios, Juan."

Gus disconnected the call and laughed heartily. Although El Animal had a vicious cunning that helped him rise to the top, it was Gus's quiet, behind the scenes planning that had ensured his cousin's success. He would be the architect of an expanded and more efficient GDM, but first he had some local problems to resolve.

THREE

Miller Residence, Franklin
9:30 P.M.

As was his custom, Chief Miller walked into his living room and settled into his favorite chair at precisely 9:30 PM. He set a cup of decaf coffee, black with one sugar, on the coffee table in front of him. Beside that, he placed the TV remote control so that it would be handy when it was time to turn on the 10 PM local newscast. This was his routine, and he permitted nothing and no one to interrupt it.

This was Miller's time to relax, catch up on the day's events and share his innermost thoughts and fears with Maggy, his wife of thirty years. As long as he had known her, she had comforted him through tough times and provided him with sage advice, keeping him grounded when he might otherwise have lost perspective. Tonight, Miller would share his thoughts with her, but she would not respond. Maggy had died two months earlier after a brief but painful struggle with ovarian cancer. Miller shook his head as if to clear those memories away and focused on a picture frame on the end table next to her favorite chair. It was oriented so that it faced him, and contained an 8" x 10" portrait of Maggy taken during their honeymoon. When he looked at the picture he could feel her presence.

Miller leaned forward and picked up a small stack of papers that included airline tickets and travel brochures, flipped though it slowly, and sadly tossed it back on the coffee table. He and Maggy had been frugal during their marriage. When they realized six months ago that their investments had grown far larger than expected, they decided to splurge and take a dream trip to Europe for their thirtieth anniversary. He remembered how excited they were when they purchased tickets for an Air France flight to Paris, and they talked about how great it was that they were taking the trip of a lifetime while they were still young and healthy enough to enjoy it.

The excitement ended, and the nightmare began, a month later when a visit to her doctor for what they thought was a routine stomach bug instead turned out to be stage four ovarian cancer. The "silent killer," they called it. It came out of nowhere, and before he could even comprehend what was happening she was gone. He shuddered at the memory of how the cancer decimated her body. She underwent surgery to remove the tumors that had spread through her abdomen, followed by a series of painful chemotherapy treatments. There was a brief period of false hope as the "CA 125" blood marker that indicated ovarian cancer dropped dramatically after the chemo. And then, as quickly as it had receded, the marker began to rise, and soon reached even higher levels as the tumor returned with a vengeance. Adding to the pain, the growing tumor constantly produced a brown, toxic fluid that periodically filled her abdomen to the point that it looked like she would surely burst until the doctors inserted a long needle and drained it, as if it were spent oil from a car. And now she was lying in the Franklin cemetery.

The Miller's only child, an adult son, returned from his home in California for the funeral and stayed a few days in a vain attempt to comfort his father. But there was nothing that he could do about the fact his father's world had crumbled, and he soon returned home. Chief Miller began the process of healing and learning how to live alone after having his life happily intertwined with Maggy's for so many years. Miller quickly realized that he had the choice between crawling into a bottle of scotch or throwing himself into his work; after draining several bottles, he chose the latter. His colleagues on the force understood when he showed up every morning at 7 AM and was often seen working until well into the night. That will pass, they thought, but it's too soon.

Miller told Maggy and about his argument with the Mayor this morning, and how that was nothing compared to the battle that they would have tomorrow morning. *I guess I should have told the bastard about our latest crime victim, but I just didn't want to hear his whiny little voice telling me how to do my job and demanding that I make the problem go away. I'll deal with him tomorrow.* In his mind he could hear her calming voice telling him not to get worked up over that sad little man.

After leaving the Mayor's office this morning, Miller heard a radio call for assistance from one of his officers and decided to respond. When he arrived at the scene on Spring Street, he learned that an anonymous source had reported that a man and a woman had stuffed what appeared to be a human body in the trunk of a car parked next to a ramshackle house. The responding officer observed bloodstains on the driveway and called for backup. From there a sordid tale unfolded.

Chief Miller turned on the television just as the 10 PM TV5 news began, guessing correctly that the drug-related murder would be the lead story. For the past week, he had followed a series of reports on the opioid crisis in western Pennsylvania by an up-and-coming TV5 investigative reporter by the name of Mercedes Boone, and her focus now seemed to be on Franklin.

When he glanced at the TV, Miller saw the twenty-something reporter standing in front of the Franklin Police Department and unmuted the TV so that he could hear the story. A solemn-looking anchor with a serious tone began, "Our lead story this evening is another drug-related murder in Franklin. Award-winning TV5 reporter Mercedes Boone has been leading TV5's investigation into the western Pennsylvania opioid crisis, and is with us live from Franklin."

Mercedes, dressed in a heavy coat with the blue TV5 logo and with her long blond hair blowing in the wind, paused briefly and then began:

"Thank you, Bill. We've just learned that a bizarre drug-related murder took place in Franklin late this morning. Our sources tell us that police received an anonymous report that two people had stuffed what looked like a human body into the trunk of a car. An officer responded and observed bloodstains where the car had been parked, and police quickly obtained a warrant to search the house. Once inside, they found a frying pan that was covered with what appeared to be human blood as well as patches of human scalp and hair."

The video shifted to a picture of the home on Spring Street, with yellow "crime scene" tape cordoning off the area, as the reporter continued,

"In a fortunate break, another Franklin police officer reportedly observed a car matching the witness' description driving along an isolated stretch of Water Works Road in Franklin, where the road runs along French Creek. Multiple police cars responded, and they discovered a man and a woman, both in their mid-twenties, pouring gasoline on the body of a deceased female and preparing to light the body on fire."

"Police arrested the two suspects, and we understand that they obtained a murder confession. Our source tells us that the victim, a female also in her twenties, was a drug runner who apparently had tried to short the couple on heroin that they had purchased. The man allegedly beat the victim to death with a frying pan while the woman – who we are told is six months pregnant – held her. The couple then allegedly hauled the body to Water Works Road, where they planned to incinerate the body in order to destroy the evidence."

The video shifted back to Mercedes.

"The two alleged murderers are being held without bond tonight in the Venango County jail. The

Franklin police department has yet to make an official statement, and has not responded to our request for information. We'll provide further details as they become available. Back to you, Bill."

The anchor asked, "Mercedes, is there any indication that this murder is related to the Sunday night murder in Franklin?"

"That's a good question, Bill. Although my sources tell me that they haven't found any direct connection between the murders, both appear to be drug related. As part of our ongoing series on the western Pennsylvania opioid crisis, TV5 is continuing its in-depth investigation in the Franklin drug situation and we'll provide further information as it becomes available."

Chief Miller chuckled as he thought, *yep, score one for Mercedes.* Although the Franklin PD had not issued a statement about this morning's murder, he assumed that one of his officers had talked to Mercedes on "background." *It's actually pretty funny to watch her manipulate my clueless young studs. She's really something to watch when she bats her doe-like brown eyes and flashes a dazzling smile at one of them. But behind those eyes is a sharp intellect – she's really nailing it. Well, no harm done, really, if the details of this murder get out. We've got a solid confession, a witness and the physical evidence. I'll just have to deal with that jackass Kelliher pissing and moaning and telling me how to do my job. After two murders in two days, he's going to come off the rails.*

Miller turned off the TV, picked up his cell phone, and slowly began counting. He had reached twenty-six when the phone rang, and after looking at the incoming number and allowing the phone to ring five times, he held it away from his ear and said "Good evening Mayor . . . yes, I saw the news report . . . yes, I know that makes you look bad . . . yes, I'll see you first thing in the morning. No, Mayor, I don't think it's funny." Miller started to ask what time the Mayor planned to arrive at his office when he realized that Kelliher had hung up on him.

Miller turned off the TV, softly kissed the picture of Maggy and headed off to bed.

SECTION III
MAKING CHOICES

ONE

Bleakley Avenue, Franklin
Tuesday, December 19
7 A.M.

Nicole Longworth was mature beyond her eleven years. She had awoken this morning in what served as her bedroom, a dirty mattress laid on the floor in a corner of the living room. She had carefully arranged an old sheet, something that she had found in a trash bin one day on her way home from school, to provide herself with some small degree of privacy. This area was her refuge, but a threadbare piece of fabric could hardly shield her from the human depravity that regularly unfolded in the small apartment.

Bleakley Avenue was no place for a child. It was on the fringe of Third Ward, an area where life somehow seemed more tenuous than elsewhere in Franklin. Drugs were dealt regularly from many of the surrounding houses, with business being particularly brisk when the monthly welfare payments arrived. The two-story building in which Nicole's apartment was located was marked by peeling paint, rotting wood and more than its share of broken windows. A rusting and abandoned 2005 PT Cruiser sat on concrete blocks in front of the building, its wheels and other salvageable parts long since stolen.

Nicole pulled her long red hair off of her freckled face, rubbed the sleep from her eyes and looked around the apartment warily for signs of what the day might bring. She noted that the door to the bedroom was closed and assumed, with good reason, that her mother and her boyfriend were sleeping off the effects of last night's partying. That was a good thing; if Nicole hurried she could leave for school and avoid the beating that her mother might inflict if she was in a bad mood. Her mother usually was in a bad mood, and Nicole always bore the brunt of it.

As she continued her survey of the apartment, Nicole noted that some fast food wrappings had been carelessly tossed on the floor and had attracted the roaches that infested the apartment. She knew that would anger her mother, so she quickly cleaned the mess up. Next, she saw several small wax packets – she had learned that they were "stamp bags" containing a single dose of heroin and that she was never to touch them – on the battered coffee table along with a spoon and a hypodermic needle. That was unusual, since her mother usually hid her needle and bags in the bedroom. Nicole hated what happened when her mother used drugs but there was nothing she could do about it.

Despite her upbringing Nicole was a fastidious girl. She thought that her neat appearance, carefully cultivated despite her meager thrift shop wardrobe, concealed from outsiders the circumstances in which she lived. She was mistaken. Nicole was popular with her classmates, and a couple of her closer friends had taken to giving her some decent articles of clothing that "they didn't need anymore." But for their kindness, she would have worn the same threadbare clothes every day.

Nicole's fantasy was to live like the other kids at school, with their normal families and comfortable, welcoming homes. When she was invited to visit one of her classmate's homes it seemed like a glimpse into a different world. Sometimes at night she dreamed of sitting down to a nicely set table and having a normal meal accompanied by pleasant conversation. That she could only dream about, however, as her reality was both depressingly different and unchangeable.

She smiled at the thought of school. Nicole liked the intellectual challenge and typically earned 'A's in all of her classes. Had her mother ever bothered to visit the school, Nicole's teachers would have told her that her daughter was unusually gifted in math and had a bright future ahead of her. Not that her mother would have cared.

Nicole sighed deeply and then decided that her first task this morning would be to clean off the coffee table, before she checked to see if there was anything that she could eat for breakfast. From hard experience she knew that breakfast was unlikely. At least she would get a free lunch at school.

After clearing the trash from the coffee table, Nicole became curious and picked up one of the stamp bags. What was it about the contents of this little bag that brought such misery into her life? As she lifted the bag she noticed, too late, that it was torn and some of the white powder that it contained spilled onto her hand. If her mother discovered that Nicole had touched her drugs, she would fly into a rage. Nicole carefully scraped the powder from her hand back into the bag. That done, she unconsciously put her hand to her mouth and bit down on a knuckle. It was an odd quirk, something that she did when she felt stress. Nicole decided to put the bag back on the table and pretend that she hadn't touched anything.

Nicole continued to get ready for school and had just started to put her coat on when she started to feel dizzy. She sat for a moment, thinking that it was probably because dinner last night had consisted of only an apple that she had brought home from school, and then started to have trouble breathing. After a moment of terror she collapsed, and as she fell her head hit the table and opened a cut that seeped bright red blood. That wound didn't matter. The white powder residue on her hand had entered her system, gradually slowed her respiration and soon her heart simply stopped beating.

Two hours later Nicole's mother walked out of the bedroom and saw her lifeless body. In response to a chilling scream the boyfriend raced out of the bedroom and, seeing what had happened, called 9-1-1. The ambulance arrived within 5 minutes, but there was nothing to be done. Matt Riley walked into the apartment as the paramedic was covering Nicole's body while the mother screamed, "My baby, my baby."

TWO

Venango County Jail
Wednesday, December 20
6 A.M.

Cody had endured a long, restless night. Each time that he drifted off to sleep, the haunting scream jolted him awake. The dream was always the same – his terrified girlfriend pleaded with him to leave the parking lot, but he ignored her. A man appeared out of the swirling snow and approached his car. And then the scream and sudden blackness. After his heartbeat settled down, he tried to piece together what had happened. It just didn't make sense.

He had been in the jail cell since the previous afternoon, when a deputy sheriff burst into his hospital room and snarled, "Get your ass out of bed and get dressed, Ware, we're going to take a little ride over to the county jail. You'll like it, there are lots of nice people just like you. Now move it, we don't have all goddamned day."

The deputy removed the handcuffs that had tethered him to the bed and, when Cody stood up, handed him his street clothes. After Cody dressed, the deputy spun him around, handcuffed his arms behind his back, and led him outside to a waiting police car.

Cody felt the bile rise in his throat as he stood next to the car and realized that his life was now totally out of his control. The deputy roughly shoved him into the back seat and the door slammed shut with an ominous thud. As Cody settled in, a wave of pain shot through his wrists and his hands began to go numb from the too-tight handcuffs. Cody squirmed briefly, seeking relief from the pain, and finally found some slight comfort when he bent forward and rested his head against the front seat.

Cody began to panic during the fifteen-minute ride to the county jail. When they arrived at the fortress-like, two-story granite jailhouse, the police car pulled into a receiving bay in the rear and a steel door immediately closed loudly behind it. The deputy pulled him out of the car, and then guided him through a steel-barred door that closed behind him with a metallic clang. Cody found himself in a small room where a jailer sat at a desk with a metal "INTAKE" sign above it, where the necessary paperwork was completed and his fingerprints and mug shot taken. Cody declined the opportunity to use the phone call, since nobody really cared enough about him to take his call.

Although Cody was no stranger to the wrong side of the law, this was his first time in a jail. He had just allowed himself to think that jail might not be as bad as he feared when he was led to another room where there was a second deputy. After being forced to provide blood and urine samples so that they could determine whether drugs were in his system, the deputy informed him that he was going to perform a 'jail' search and ordered Cody to remove all of his clothes.

He winced as the deputy, using a flashlight, closely

examined his entire body. Just when Cody thought that the search was over, the deputy ordered, "Stand over that mirror on the floor and squat."

Cody was stunned, and turned to face the deputy. "What the hell? I'm not going to do that. What kind of sicko are you?"

The deputy calmly said, "Your call, Ware, either do what I tell you or you'll get a medical examination where they'll probe into all of those hard to reach parts of your body. I guarantee that you won't like that." Near tears from the humiliation, Cody did as he was told.

"Now cough," the deputy ordered. Cody was briefly confused, and then realized that the point of this was to dislodge any contraband – drugs – that he may have hidden in his anus. *Who in their right mind would hide drugs there? Christ, that would be damned uncomfortable, and I've heard that people have died when the drugs leaked into their system.*

"OK, now stand up," the deputy ordered. Another deputy tossed Cody a well-worn orange prison jumpsuit made from a coarse wool material, along with a pair of far-too-large plastic sandals, one of which was missing a heel. After that, he was led to another room where he was required to take a shower, but allowed only ninety seconds of cold water to complete the task.

Cody was brought to a cell that had a two-level steel bunk bed. "You're out of luck, Ware, we don't have any mattresses right now, but we should be able to give you one in the morning. From the looks of things, you're going to be with us for a while." The jailer closed the door behind him, leaving Cody to settle into his new home.

The first thing that Cody noticed about the cell was the

sound of someone loudly snoring in the top bunk, and then his senses were assaulted by an overpowering stench of body odor. He desperately wanted to flee, but that was not an option. He was confined in a six by eight foot cage. Aside from the bed, the cell contained a stainless steel combination toilet and sink, and a metal mirror against the rear wall. He shuddered at the thought that there would be no privacy when he used the toilet.

Cody spread the two thin woolen blankets that he had been issued on the lower bunk and sat down. After a while he stretched out on the bed and tried to calm himself. Exhaustion finally overtook him around 5 AM, but a half hour later a harsh burst of fluorescent light jarred him awake. His first conscious thought was that he was chilled to the bone. His body ached from the hardness of the steel bunk bed, and as he began to stretch his aching muscles it slowly registered that he had a throbbing headache and mild chills.

The hospital had given him medication to ease his heroin withdrawal, but a deputy seemed to take a sadistic pleasure in confiscating it during the intake process, "Sorry, jail policy, no can do." The dose that he has taken in the hospital had worn off. A sudden wave of nausea sent him scuttling to the toilet.

His stomach now purged, Cody sat on the cold cell floor with his head in his hands and began to sob. *How the hell did I sink this low?* A cough interrupted his thoughts and Cody turned to see that staring down at him from the top bunk was a large, muscular man in his early thirties with long, greasy brown hair, a greying beard and a badly bruised right eye that had swollen shut.

"That's disgusting, man. Come in my cell and puke all over the place. Now you're crying like a girl. I knew you were trouble when they put you in here. Maybe a good ass-kicking will teach you some manners."

Cody watched his cellmate climb down from the top bunk, and he slowly backed up against the far wall as the man approached him. He felt his stomach constrict, and broke into a cold sweat as the realization dawned on him that the man was even larger and tougher than he had first appeared. Cody smelled his foul breath as the man closed to within six inches of him and stared down at the bandage on his face.

"What the fuck happened to your face, boy? Been stickin' your nose where it didn't belong?"

"Some dude shot me." Cody coughed and then laughed nervously. "Guess he didn't like the music I was playing. Shit happens, right?"

His cellmate glared at him for a moment, and then snarled, "Seems like a waste of a bullet. Little dude like you, I'd just stomp your ass."

Cody tried to defuse the situation with a little humor. "Nah, you wouldn't want to get your shoes dirty stomping on me. Besides, once you get to know me I'm sure you'll like me. So, my man, what do they call you?"

"Some people call me Tiny, but you don't call me nothing, asshole." A sudden knee to the crotch doubled Cody over. He never saw the punch that knocked him unconscious and popped several of the stitches that had closed the bullet wound on the side of his head.

Tiny grabbed Cody and pushed his face against the rim of the toilet, laughing as he visualized knocking Cody's teeth out of his mouth when he kicked him in the back of the head. Tiny began to raise his leg for a vicious kick when he heard a shouted order from just outside the cell. "Freeze. Now step back against your bunk."

Tiny paused just long enough to process that interruption, then scoffed, "Or what, you gonna send me to prison?" He turned his attention back to Cody, again raising his leg to prepare for a kick, when he felt a stinging sensation in his back as a Taser dart struck him between his shoulder blades. The Taser's 50,000 volts of electricity disrupted his nervous system, and his body went rigid and then collapsed and landed next to Cody.

The cell door swung open and two officers entered the cell. Tiny felt his arms being yanked roughly behind him, and heard a metallic snap as handcuffs were fastened on his wrist. One of the officers grunted as he lifted Tiny and dragged him toward the cell door. The second officer, after keying his radio and calling for assistance, bent over Cody and examined his injuries.

"Looks like he'll be OK once they stitch him up again, he's not bleeding too bad. I wonder what the hell this was all about. I busted this guy a couple of days ago, and he didn't seem like the violent type to me."

Cody's eyes fluttered open and he looked up at Officer Matt Riley. "We gotta stop meeting like this, Matt."

"You are a shit magnet, Cody. What happened here?"

"I thought you cops were supposed to be observant. Man Mountain over there just beat the crap out of me."

"Not funny, Cody. If I hadn't checked on you, either you'd be dead right now or at least in serious need of a dentist. Ol'

Tiny looked like he was just about to finish the job. Let's get you to the infirmary so that they can sew you back together again. Here, hold this compress on your head so you don't bleed all over the place. That would really piss off Tiny. Can you stand up or do we need to get you a wheel chair?"

"Yeah, I'm good, man, just help me up."

Cody grabbed Matt's outstretched hand and slowly rose to his feet. "I'm OK. I can walk."

Matt caught Cody as his knees buckled and said, "Sure you can. Let's have you sit on your bunk for a few minutes before we get you to the infirmary. That was a pretty solid hit that you took, and I don't think you're quite ready to walk." Matt leaned in towards Cody and lowered his voice, "Besides, I want to talk with you a bit. That's why I stopped by here at the end of my shift."

"We're going to talk in here?"

"No, your new neighbors will hear us. And what I have to say I don't want anyone else to hear. So, when you're feeling OK let's take a walk."

After stopping at the infirmary to repair the broken stiches, Matt led Cody to a small interior room that featured only a gray metal desk bolted to the floor and two gray metal chairs. Waving Cody into one of the chairs, Matt sat on the table in front of Cody and looked down at him.

"You look like shit, you know that?"

"Tell me something I don't know."

"OK, Cody, I'll tell you some things that you probably haven't figured out yet. You've dug yourself a really deep hole, man. You're looking at 8 to 10 years in state prison if you're lucky. Right now, we've got a previous warrant out on you for possession. Add to that child endangerment – for Christ sakes, Cody, bringing a kid on a drug buy! What the hell were you two thinking? And since you put the little girl in a situation where her mother was murdered right in front of her, you can bet that the prosecutor is going to seek the max sentence from a very sympathetic judge, and there won't be any plea bargain on this one."

Matt gestured at their surroundings and said, "You've only been here in county jail overnight, and you can see that it's no picnic. What happened to you this morning may not happen all the time, but it does happen. And when the word gets around – and it will – about what you exposed that little girl to, there'll be a few other folks taking a run at you just for sport."

Matt pushed himself off the table and stood in front of Cody, "And if you think this place is bad, it's the minor leagues compared to what you're gonna find in the state pen. The conditions there really suck, and you'll be in with a bunch of career criminals that are there for the long-term. Don't be surprised if one of them thinks you're kinda cute. And if you think that any of the guards there will really give a crap about what happens to you, you're wrong."

Cody winced as he watched a large roach crawl down the wall behind Matt. *A night in this county jail is about as bad as I'd like to experience, and he's talking about a long-term stay in an even bigger shithole. Or, maybe he's just blowing some smoke to scare me. I bet a good lawyer will have me on the street in a couple of days and get most of the charges tossed. There's got to be some way out of this.*

"Before we cut to the chase on our little chat, there's one

more piece of information that I want you to think about. Yesterday I responded to a call over in Third Ward. Seems that there was an 11-year-old child whose mother found her unresponsive when she finally woke up after a hard night of partying. I got there just as the paramedic gave up on trying to revive the kid. An eleven-year-old little girl, Cody. She was a cute little kid, long red hair and freckles. From what I heard, she minded her own business and was doing well in school despite the way she was growing up. And do you know what happened? The kid was playing in the squalid little pig sty that her mother called an apartment and she came in contact with some new heroin brand that her mother had left out in the open – Ace of Diamonds I think they called it." Matt slammed his fist on the table, and the sound reverberated through the room. "And just by being exposed to the damn stuff she went into cardiac arrest and died."

Cody recoiled at the sound of Matt's hand slamming into the table and the anger that was boiling over from deep inside him. On one level, Cody recognized that Matt was just a decent guy who cared about other people and wanted to protect them from something that he saw as evil and dangerous. On a different level, Cody saw Matt as clueless. This was just the way things were, and there's nothing he could do to change that. "I don't know what to say, Matt. I don't doubt any of what you're saying. But what the hell can I do about any of it?"

"Cody, it's time for you to make a good decision for a change. I want the bastards that are responsible for bringing this shit into Franklin. I'm not naïve enough to think that I can stop it, or that taking one person out of the drug trade will even slow it down much. But, damn it, I want to put a dent in it. To do that, I need your help."

"Whoa, Matt, there's nothing that I could do to help you, and why the hell would I get involved with something like that anyway? You know what the dealers are like. If I crossed them I'd be a dead man."

"And if you do nothing, you'll be in the state pen for 8 to 10 years, maybe longer if you draw an ornery judge. with a bunch of people who'll entertain themselves by beating the crap out of you. Trust me on this, Cody, you won't survive there."

Cody knew that Matt was right but wasn't willing to concede the point. "I don't see any better options."

Matt said, "Here's what I've been thinking. We need someone to get close to the guys that are bringing this Ace of Diamonds into Franklin. We know who the little guys are, and we pick them off when we get a chance. But I want to find out who's really behind this and nail his ass. So I'm suggesting that when you talk with Elliot Finkleman, Esquire – who even by typical lowly lawyer standards is a sleazy asshole, by the way – you tell him that I mentioned the possibility that you could become a confidential informant. After you discuss it with your esteemed legal counsel, presuming that you can find him sober, you can decide if you want to talk more about it. I can't promise you anything without going to the DA, but this may be your last chance, Cody."

THREE

Myron Foley was a creature of habit. He was a nocturnal animal, sleeping away most of the day and rising early in the evening to begin his routine. At 9 P.M. he would step out of his apartment onto the front porch and light a Swisher Sweet "Outlaw." Myron would leisurely savor the cigar, and the brief period of peace while it lasted, before he took to the streets to ply his trade.

Tonight, for a change, was a relatively warm night and Myron was wearing a light jacket. Although the streetlights near his house had long since been burned out – the city employees tasked with replacing the lights were very reluctant to do so in this part of town – there was a full moon that provided sufficient light to see that there was someone sitting in a strange car in front of his house. *That doesn't look right. I wonder who the hell that is in the car?*

As Myron flicked open the top of his vintage Ronson lighter, a memento of the father that he never knew, and thumbed the wheel to ignite the flame, he sensed the presence of someone sitting on a chair behind him. *What the hell? I didn't see anyone there when I came out here. Not that I could*

61

see anyone in that dark corner. I'm just being paranoid. He slowly turned around and found himself staring down the barrel of a sawed-off shotgun held by an unwelcome visitor.

"Hello, MF. I wouldn't make any sudden moves if I was you."

"Tony, you ignorant fucking wop, that ain't funny. If you don't put that goddamned cannon away you're going to eat it. What the hell are you up to?"

"You know, I read somewhere that if you fired one of these close up you could actually blow a hole clear through a human body. No shit, the size you could put your fist through. Now that sounds kinda unlikely, but I've always wanted to try it and find out. You're a big son-of-a-bitch though, so it probably wouldn't be a fair test. But I'm guessing it would still fuck you up pretty good."

"Tony, damn it, put the piece down."

"MF, we have a little problem, you and I. Now, before we get into that, I guess I ought to tell you that this thing has a hair-trigger and my finger is already resting on it. So it wouldn't really be in your interest to make me nervous, if you catch my drift. Although, since I'm more than a little pissed at you, that would kinda make my day. Do we understand each other?"

"You've made your point, Tony. So just what the fuck is this all about?"

"How about you and I take a ride and talk about it. See that red Charger parked out front? You just walk real slow to the front passenger seat and strap yourself in. And don't worry about feeling lonely - I'll be sitting right behind you."

Myron hesitated, recognizing that he had two options, both of them bad. If he tried to run he would die right here on his porch. Not good. The likely result of going for a ride with Tony is that he would die somewhere else. *Fuck it, I'll go for the ride and see if he makes a mistake. And if he does, I'll break every bone in his greasy little body.* He walked to the car, sat down and strapped himself in.

Tony took his position in the back seat, directly behind Myron, and spoke to the driver. "Head out Ajax Road, past the old VHI plant, and find us a nice quiet place by the river where we can have a friendly chat."

The driver silently nodded and pulled away from the curb.

"So, MF, let me explain our little problem to you. Seems that the boss wasn't real happy about you offing that girl in the car the other night. That's going to bring us a lot of unwanted attention from the cops and reporters, and that's bad for business. That cute little reporter on the TV5 news is already picking up the trail. And the way the boss put it to me was that I gotta fix this little problem right fucking now. So, I decided to have a little chat with you. I don't really want to think about what will happen if I don't clean this up. So, how do you suppose we're gonna do that?"

"Tony, we can fix this. But you gotta understand what happened. The bitch showed up with another guy and my daughter. What would you do if it was your girlfriend and kid?"

"MF, what I'd do just doesn't matter. The boss is pissed and I gotta make him happy. So just shut the fuck up and think about how we fix this."

They drove in silence past an abandoned VHI plant whose peeling paint and broken windows testified to several years of neglect. The plant's security lights revealed several abandoned and rusting trailers scattered across a parking lot that was gradually being reclaimed by weeds. MF felt a chill down his spine as the plant's lights faded into the distance and they were engulfed in total darkness.

The driver ignored a large sign that warned that they were entering private property and continued onto a narrow gravel road that cut through a heavily wooded area. As the car lurched over the rough road MF thought he could see occasional reflections of the headlights on the surface of the river that he knew must be somewhere to his left, but saw no signs of human activity. *Christ, you could dump a body down here and no one would ever find it. Aw, shit. I guess that tells me all I need to know about how this little joy ride is going to end.* MF carefully eyed the driver and thought about punching him and jumping out of the car. As he fingered the seat belt buckle he remembered that Tony had a shotgun pointed at his back, and decided to wait for a better opportunity.

They continued down Ajax Road for about five minutes without seeing any sign of life, other than the occasional rodent that scurried across the road in front of them, until the driver found the spot that he was looking for and pulled over. In the glow of the headlights, MF could see there was a large boulder about 10 feet from the edge of the road, and the river was just beyond that. The driver turned to Tony and in a deep, gravelly voice with a peculiar accent said, "This is the place. No one's going to bother us here." There was something about that voice that sent chills through both Tony and MF.

The headlights went out and they were enveloped in darkness. Tony waited a minute until his eyes adjusted to the darkness and then prodded MF with the barrel of his shotgun. "Out of the car and walk towards the river. Let's finish our little talk."

MF stepped out of the car and found that the moonlight was sufficient to find his way. The only sounds were the gurgling of the river and the intermittent croaking of a frog. The driver walked silently behind him, and Tony was to his right. MF stopped and turned towards Tony, "Man, I know I fucked up, but I can make it right. How about I talk to your boss and explain it to him?"

"MF, you ain't ever gonna know who the boss is, much less meet him. You're at the bottom of the food chain. The only reason I'm even talking to you, and that you even know who I am, is that we grew up together and our families are tight. I figured I owe you that much. But don't press your luck. All you had to do was sell the shit that we provided and not do something stupid. And man, did you do something stupid."

"How about you just let me take the fall? I'll confess, tell the cops that I followed Brandi and that dipshit boyfriend of hers and lost my cool. They'll believe it. Hell, that's why I shot them. It wasn't about drugs. It was personal. Real personal."

"I don't know, MF, that could work, but the problem is that the cops know that place where you shot those two is a drug mart. You gotta come up with something better than that. You got some better ideas, I'm listening."

"We can make it work, Tony. Look, I can go to the cops and tell that I found out Brandi was screwing around and I lost my temper. I saw them on the road and forced them into the parking lot and shot them. They know that Brandi and me were together because she called them on me a couple of times when she stepped out of line and I had to smack her around a bit." *This is not going well. Either I make my move now or I'm a dead man.*

"Maybe, MF. Let me think about whether Mr. A...., I mean the boss, would buy that."

A subtle change in MF's body language, signaling something between fear and determination, alerted Tony that MF was about to try something. Tony's instinct was confirmed a second later as MF lunged toward him. The report of the shotgun firing echoed across the river as MF fell to the ground.

Tony turned to the driver and laughed as he said, "Just like I thought, that crap about blowing a clean hole through a body was bullshit. But it sure made a hell of a mess. Help me drag him to the river so we can throw his dead ass in."

Tony put down his shotgun and grabbed an arm, the driver wordlessly grabbed the other arm and together they dragged MF's corpse to the edge of the water. As Tony prepared to throw the body in the river, the driver turned to him.

"I just remembered, the boss had a message he wanted me to give you."

Angrily, Tony turned to the driver. "And you just now remembered? How fucking dumb are you? You know I'm already on thin ice. What did Gus have to say?"

The driver raised a pistol that he had concealed behind his back, pointed it at Tony's head and fired two rounds. "He said your services are no longer required."

FOUR

Few things in life are more depressing than having only two choices, both of them bad. Cody could choose to roll the dice on going to trial on multiple criminal charges, with the likelihood that he would receive a lengthy prison sentence. Or, he could choose to become a CI and maybe walk free, but with the risk that he would die for betraying a drug dealer.

Cody was pondering those choices as the morning jail routine began. At 5:30 AM the lights snapped on and jolted him awake, and soon the routine prison clatter began. A guard slid a tray into his cell that contained a breakfast of runny, undercooked eggs, greasy bacon and a moldy English muffin. Cody picked at the food, leaving half of it uneaten, and laid back on his bed.

Because his usual pastime, texting his friends and surfing the net, was not an option, he had nothing to do but dwell on the chain of events that landed him in jail. When the absurdity of his situation finally hit him Cody had to laugh. "Unfreaking believable. Only in Franklin!"

From just outside his cell Cody heard Matt's voice, "I'm

glad that you can find something funny, given your present circumstances. If I were you, I think I'd be scared shitless right about now." Cody glared at him defiantly and slow-ly gave him the finger. "OK, fine, I see that I haven't gotten through to you." Matt grabbed him by the arm and pulled him off of the bunk. "Come on, let's take a walk."

When Matt and Cody reached the same room where they had talked yesterday, Cody said, "Hey, Matt. Now, you've got to admit, there is an element of humor in all of this. I'm sitting in jail facing hard time while you cops do your best to screw me over. And I'm the guy that got shot, remember? Now you want me to be a CI and save the world from the evil drug dealers? You're supposed to be the super-stud ex-Marine. You go save the fucking world and risk your ass. All I want is to do a little dope and chill out."

A visibly angered Matt snapped back, "Bullshit, Cody. There's nothing funny about this. And if you're thinking of some clever, smart-ass remark, you might want to consider that I tend to have a bad temper when people insult me."

Almost disdainfully, Cody responded, "Come on, Matt, stop living in your fantasy world. Whatever I do, I'm fucked. Either I spend a big chunk of my life in prison, or I roll the dice on the CI thing and probably get my ass blown away by a dealer. Even if they don't get to me right away, I'll have to spend the rest of my life looking over my shoulder. And, however it plays out, the dealers keep making money and you cops put in your eight hour days, go home to your nice little houses and count down the time until you draw a pension. "

"I'm not going to argue with you, Cody. Let's get down to it. Did you talk with Finkleman about becoming a CI?"

"Yeah, and he thinks it's a really dumb idea. The way he put it to me, there's no real upside, and a man could get his ass blown away just for thinking those kinds of thoughts."

"And what do you think, Cody?"

"It's pretty simple. Spare me the goody two shoes, save the world bullshit. What's in it for me? Make it worth my while – and by that I mean I don't want to spend any more time in the county slammer, much less state prison – and we may have something to talk about. If not, you can just kiss my ass."

"Fair enough, that's pretty blunt. So, I've talked to the DA. If you work with us as a CI, *and* if we get a good bust of some of the serious players, we'll dismiss everything but the child endangerment charges. So, you're looking at no jail time on the drug charges. You'll have to take your chances with the judge on the child endangerment charge, but the DA will ask for probation. But, no bust and no deal. And if you step one inch outside of the lines we draw for you, no deal."

Cody bit down on his lower lip and looked thoughtful for a moment before saying, "Let me think about it."

"Okay. I'll be back this afternoon, and I'll need your answer."

FIVE

Augustine's Ristorante
10 A.M.

Gus Amoroso chuckled as he replaced his coffee cup in its matching china saucer sitting on his desk. A newly arrived guest, seeing no need to knock, had simply walked into Gus' office, sat down, and was staring at him through intense blue eyes. The man was just under six feet tall, with a powerful athletic build, and elegantly dressed. Gus knew from long experience that his guest would silently continue to stare until something prompted him to speak. Even then, the man would only mutter a few quiet words. *If I didn't know better, just looking at him I'd think he was a male model. Well, except for that 4-inch scar on the left side of his face and a glare that can freeze you dead in your tracks.*

Although the man had worked for him for almost ten years, Gus did not know his real name and simply thought of him as "Driver." That was not a mark of disrespect, however, for over time Driver had become one of Gus' most trusted and valued business associates. The nickname had originated when Gus' regular driver called in sick, and out of necessity one of Augustine's busboys had been pressed into service. Grudgingly accepting the necessity of a replacement driver,

Gus asked the man his name but the response, given in a quiet voice coupled with a heavy eastern European accent, was unintelligible. So, Gus just settled for calling him Driver, and that suited them both just fine.

Early in their relationship, Gus had discovered that Driver had a unique skill: he could make problems – and usually the people that were causing them – disappear. Permanently. To this day, Gus had no idea where Driver came from, how he acquired his skills or, for that matter, what those skills really were. But Gus was not one to argue with success, and he had learned to just tell Driver about a problem that he wanted solved and then stay out of his way.

"Good morning, Driver. I trust you have some news to share with me concerning our little problem in Franklin?"

"Yes."

"And perhaps you would be so kind as to tell me what has happened?"

Driver snickered. "The problem is fixed."

Gus smiled insincerely and said, "Well, that is good news. Will the authorities find any bodies?"

"Yes."

Gus was visibly startled. One of Driver's trademarks was that "problems" tended to just disappear, leaving nothing behind but a mystery. Gus took a moment to control his rising anger. "Do you think that was a good idea, Driver? Won't that draw unwanted attention to us?"

"No."

"Well, Driver, I find it hard to believe that the police are going to find two dead bodies . . ." Gus paused as a thought occurred to him, "there were only two, right?" Driver nodded.

"And not at least suspect that it may have something to do with our business activities."

Driver's lips curled into a faint, but chilling, smile. "Not a problem."

"From the look in your eyes I suspect there will be an element of humor in all of this. Am I correct?"

Driver's face broke into a broader grin. "Oh, yes. You'll laugh your ass off."

Gus had seen that look before, and it caused him to relax. "Driver, you've never disappointed me. So, enough of that, we seem to have another problem that needs to be dealt with."

Driver looked at Gus and raised a questioning eyebrow.

"I understand that there is a young cop in Franklin – an ex-Marine – who's starting to nose around in our business. We can't have that, now can we? But it is very important that, if something unfortunate should happen to this young man, no one should have any suspicion that we were involved or that it was anything other than an accident. You understand that the authorities will be very unforgiving of anyone connected with an unfortunate incident involving a cop?"

"Yes."

"Well, that takes care of our business for the day. Would you care to join me for lunch? I'm having an excellent cacciucco alla Livornese stew, paired with a nice Vernaccia di San Gimignano wine. A meal fit for the gods."

"No." And with that, Driver got up and walked out the door.

SIX

It had been nearly a month since his last nightmare. Matt moaned and thrashed, kicking his sweat-soaked sheets to the floor. In his mind's eye, he was reliving the day that he was wounded.

Matt shouted over the sounds of the developing battle. "Listen up. Campbell's down on the other side and it looks like he's hurt bad. I'm going to haul ass over there and grab him, so when I go into the canal everyone lay down a steady covering fire. Jones, we're taking heavy fire from the tree line. Put a couple of HE rounds in there with your grenade launcher."

Jones looked at Matt in disbelief and screamed, "Corporal, that's just fucking nuts. No way are you going to get through all of that fire. We need to get some reinforcements up here before we cross that canal again."

Matt glared at Jones and screamed over the sounds of the battle, "Bullshit. Campbell will be dead if we don't get off our asses and get him back over here. Just do what I told you. We're not leaving him over there." Matt slipped into the filthy canal water, and after emerging on the other side began to crawl the fifty meters to Campbell. He made his way slowly, as bullets cracked past his head and impacted on the ground nearby, peppering him with stone fragments. Covering that short distance seemed to take an eternity.

Matt finally reached Campbell and saw that he was conscious, but had a sucking chest wound and was bleeding heavily from a wound in his lower right thigh. Tensing as enemy rounds continued to impact around him, Matt applied a tourniquet to the thigh and plugged the chest wound with a battle dressing from his first aid kit. By then, Campbell had slipped into shock and was unconscious. Matt could do no more to help him where they were, so he began dragging him back towards the canal. He managed to make it half way before a rocket-propelled grenade exploded nearby, peppering him with shrapnel. Matt shook his head to clear it, and wiped blood from his eyes that was flowing from a nasty gash caused by a piece of shrapnel that had struck his forehead. Matt resumed his crawl towards the canal and had almost made it when a round clanged off his helmet, snapping his head to the side and stunning him. Matt slowly regained his senses and realized that the bullet had struck a glancing blow that had been deflected by his helmet. Although it hadn't caused any serious harm, its force had left him bruised and with a pounding headache.

Matt finally managed to drag Campbell into the canal. He relaxed briefly in the shelter of the canal bank, which shielded them from the hostile fire. His squad mates laid down a withering covering fire in an attempt to protect him, and when he sensed that the enemy fire had slackened he waded towards safety on the friendly side. Matt reached the bank and had just begun to lift Campbell out of the canal to waiting hands when he heard a sickening thud and Campbell's head exploded in a red mist and a splatter of gray matter A second later, he felt a searing pain in his left arm and lower back as he spun uncontrollably back into the water.

Matt was jolted awake by a ringing telephone. It took him a moment to fully awaken and compose himself. He reached for the phone and answered, "Hello?"

"Matt, this is Lieutenant Tucker. I need you to meet me at the DA's office right away."

Matt considered that for a moment, and decided that he resented this intrusion on his weekend. He had been through a rough stretch at work and deserved the time off. "Lieutenant, I'm kind of busy right now. This is a really bad time."

"Matt, I don't care what you're doing or who you're doing it with. I need you here in 15 minutes."

Uncharacteristically, Matt exploded. "Dammit, Lieutenant. I just got off six hours ago and hardly fell asleep before you woke me up. You know it's been a bitch of a week for me, and this is supposed to be my long weekend. Why don't you call someone else in?"

"Matt, I can't explain it to you on the phone, but this is really important and, believe it or not, you're the only one that I trust to do what has to be done. So, spare me the bullshit and get your ass down here right now. When you get here don't worry if the door is closed, just come right into the DA's office." With that, the line went dead.

Matt had second thoughts about pushing back on the Lieutenant. *Man, that's not like him, he's usually pretty laid back. I wonder what the hell is going on that has him so fired up and the DA involved? It must have something to do with*

Cody and that girl that got killed. Oh, what the hell, I better head in and see what this is about. Matt yawned and stretched as he got out of bed and put on his uniform.

Twenty minutes later Archer's secretary greeted Matt as he walked in the door, "Hi, Matt, the DA and Lieutenant Tucker are waiting for you so go on in. But I don't envy you going in there. They've really been going at it for about a half hour. What in the heck has them so worked up?"

"I haven't a clue, Rene, Tucker just told me to get down here ASAP and here I am. I guess I better go see what's going on." Matt continued walking and as he neared the closed door to the DA's office he could hear the muffled sound of Lieutenant Tucker shouting.

"I don't give a damn what you think. You may be able to get an arrest warrant, but I guarantee you that you won't find a single cop who'll execute that warrant. And you goddamn well know that."

Matt knocked and immediately opened the door. He found a red-faced Lieutenant Tucker face to face with Dennis Archer, the plump, 50ish Venango County DA. Archer enjoyed a very good reputation among the cops as a straight shooter. He wouldn't bring a bad prosecution, and he knew how to work with the police to develop a case. Unlike his predecessor, he never threw a cop under the bus to cover his own ass.

Archer was not going to back down. "Lieutenant, just what the hell do you expect me to do? We've got two dead bodies, we've found the murder weapon and we've lifted prints from that weapon. That gives us some pretty compelling evidence of who the killer was, and I can't just ignore that."

Lieutenant Tucker turned to Matt and pointed to a chair

and snarled, "Sit," and then turned back to the DA. "I came to you to help us sort through this, and I already feel like I went behind the Chief's back. I'm damn sure not going to let you take the Chief down until we get a chance to figure this out. You know as well as I do that he's innocent, and he damn sure deserves better than to be arrested and locked up like a common criminal."

"Given the circumstances, you did the right thing – hell, the only thing you could do – coming to me and you know it. I share your disbelief that the Chief was involved in this, but I've seen stranger things happen and so have you. People who you've known and respected for years, the sort of people that you'd want as role models for your kids, and then something happens that makes them go off the deep end. I'm not saying that happened here, but it might have. So we can't just ignore the evidence."

Archer paused for a minute, pursed his lips, and resumed a normal speaking voice. "OK, look, here's what I'm willing to do. If you bring me the Chief's badge and tell me that he has stepped down until the investigation is over, I'll try to buy you at least 48 hours to sort this out before I take any action. You know that the press will be all over this, as will our asshole mayor, so I'm going to be under a lot of pressure to make an arrest. I don't think I have to tell you this, but I'm on your side. If I can help you, I will. But make no mistake about this, I will *not* bend the rules and I *will* follow the evidence wherever it leads us."

"Thank you, Dennis, that at least gives us some breathing room." Lieutenant Tucker turned to Matt, "OK, you heard part of that, so let me fill you in on all of the details and then I have a job for you..."

SEVEN

Franklin Police Department
3 P.M.

Matt Riley would rather be anywhere else, doing anything else, than where he was now. He paused for a moment outside of Chief Miller's office, took a deep breath and knocked on the frame of his open door.

Miller looked up from a document that he was reading and smiled when he saw Matt. He welcomed the interruption to the administrative nonsense that he was working on. "Come on in and grab a seat, Matt. I thought you were off duty today."

"I was, but Lieutenant Tucker called me in. You heard that a jogger found two bodies on the riverbank, down by the Justus jogging trail, this morning?"

"Yeah, but I don't have any details yet. I assigned it to Tucker, but he hasn't gotten back to me. I heard that it was pretty gruesome, and the jogger is now a basket case. So, what's going on?"

Matt swallowed hard and began to answer the question while avoiding, as long as he could, the crux of the matter. "The Lieutenant told me that one of the victims was killed by a shotgun blast at point blank range. The thing is, his hands were handcuffed behind him and he was tied to the other corpse."

Miller dropped the document that he was looking at, "What the hell? That's damned unusual." Miller considered that information for a moment and then asked, "Police-type handcuffs?"

"Yeah. And the second one was shot twice in the head at close range with a 9 mm round. Right about the same time that the jogger found the bodies, a couple of kids found a Glock 9 mm out on Ajax Road, past the old VHI Plant. Tucker said that the weapon wasn't hidden; it was almost like whoever did it wanted it to be found. Ballistics matched the Glock to the bullets they took out of one of the decedents. There was also blood on the ground that matched the victims, and you could see where the bodies had been dragged to the river."

"And have we ID'd the victims?"

Matt noticeably hesitated, reluctant to answer the Chief's question, and finally said, "Not yet, they're still working on it. The victims had no identification on them."

Miller sensed Matt's discomfort, and wondered what was behind it. "Did they get prints off the weapon?"

"Yeah, Chief, they did, and they have a good match."

Impatiently, the Chief said, "Well, can we skip the suspense? Who was the shooter?"

"Chief, this makes no sense, but the prints were yours."

Chief Miller snapped at Matt. "Like hell they were. Where did you come up with that load of crap? Are you trying to tell me that I'm a suspect?"

"Chief, the gun had your prints on it, and it's the same model that you carry. We've submitted an urgent trace request to the ATF National Trace Center, but don't have anything back yet. There's no telling how long that process will take." Matt thought about what he had just said, and shook his head. "Damn, I wish it was like on TV, where they just type the serial number into a computer and a name magically pops out. Anyway, it would help if I could take a look at your pistol."

The Chief exhaled heavily and sat down. "There's a problem with that, Matt. I haven't been able to find it since Tuesday night. Last I saw it, it was in my den at home. But when I looked for it Wednesday morning before work, it wasn't there. I thought about reporting it, but it would have been a bit embarrassing for a police chief to lose his own weapon. Anyway, I've been doing some work around the house and have moved a lot of stuff, so I figure that I probably buried it under something. Did you check with our admin guy – he should have the serial number for all of the departments' weapons?"

"You'd think so, now wouldn't you, but when I checked he told me that he'd look into it and get back to me. I wouldn't hold my breath on that one. Anyway, there's got to be an explanation for this. At least show me your handcuffs so we can rule that out."

"Matt, my handcuffs were with the pistol. I don't know where they are either. I know this really looks bad, but believe me, I didn't have anything to do with the killings."

"Chief, look me in the eye and tell me that you had nothing to do with this and I'll believe you."

"Christ, Matt, you know better than that." Chief Miller looked directly at Matt with a withering glare, "OK, I had nothing to do with those murders. Satisfied?"

Matt nodded his acceptance, "Chief, I had to ask. What I think doesn't matter, though. We have a real problem on our hands. You can be sure that this will be the lead on the TV news tonight, and there'll be real pressure to arrest someone. There's a TV5 reporter focusing on the drug problem in Franklin, and she seems to have some pretty good sources. Right now, you're the leading, hell the only, suspect."

"Come on, Matt, I know that having my pistol turn up as the murder weapon doesn't exactly look good, but I'm hardly a murder suspect."

"Chief, the reason Lieutenant Tucker called me in was that he already went to the DA with this. The Lieutenant was at a loss for what to do, but given the circumstances thought he better take it to the DA without involving you. The DA about went nuts. He doesn't think you did this either, but he's faced with two corpses, a gun with your fingerprints on it and what may be your handcuffs on one of the bodies. That evidence points to you as the primary suspect for two counts of murder one. The press will be all over this, and the DA has already talked with the mayor, who wants you behind bars right now. The way I understand it, Kelliher was quite pleased when he heard the news."

"I've worked with Dennis Archer for years, and I'm sure that he won't do anything rash until we sort this out."

"Chief, Lieutenant Tucker sent me here to talk with you while he tries to calm the DA down a bit more. The Lieutenant got Archer to agree that if you voluntarily take administrative leave during the investigation he won't charge you with murder at this point, despite some pretty compelling evidence. He'll slow play it while we try to sort out what the hell happened. At least he can tell the press that you've been relieved of your duties while the investigation is ongoing. But they both wanted me to make this clear - if I don't come back with your badge in my hand and your word that you'll just drop out of sight and keep your mouth shut, the DA will get a warrant for your arrest. Once he does that, you'll be in jail, and even if a judge wanted to let you out on bail I don't think he could."

"Damn it, Matt, if I step down and don't have a chance to tell my side of the story it will look like I'm guilty."

"Chief, I'm really sorry about this, but you already look guilty. If you were still running the department our investigation would hardly look credible. Take a vacation, Chief, and we'll sort this out. Everyone in the department supports you and will bust their ass to prove that you're innocent."

Chief Miller looked down at his chest, slowly unpinned his badge and tossed it on the desk in front of Matt. The badge made a jarring metallic sound as it hit the desk and Miller glared briefly at Matt while he debated saying what was on his mind. Wordlessly, Miller stood up and walked out of his office.

EIGHT

Cody was sitting on his bunk, staring at the wall in deep thought. Although the prospect of spending time in prison terrified him, that was not his immediate problem. Whether he would be convicted and incarcerated would play out over several months as his case wound its way through the legal system. Of far more immediate concern was that the word was out on the cellblock that Tiny, his former cellmate, intended to kill him.

A chill went down his spine as Cody finally recognized that even if he were *very* careful, and *very* lucky, at most he would delay the inevitable attack. If he just had to worry about Tiny, the odds would have been in Cody's favor, since it would have been simple enough for the guards to keep the two men separated. But Cody knew that Tiny controlled a small group of prisoners, and therefore could pick a time and place for an attack that would minimize the chance that the guards could intervene. Cody didn't know how many men Tiny controlled, much less their identities.

Even as his mind ran down this path, Cody was thinking that maybe it would be best if Tiny or his colleagues succeeded. As much as he tried to excuse his actions, Cody kept coming back to the fact that the only reason that Brandi was dead – and Daisy was an orphan – was because of him. *Damn it, there was no reason to go there that night. If I had just listened to her – I don't know how, but she sensed that something was wrong and begged me to leave. But I had to be the hotshot and tell her that I had it under control. Now she's dead, and God only knows what's happened to Daisy.*

Cody's thoughts were interrupted by the sound of approaching footsteps. He looked up and saw Matt and a guard approaching his cell. Surprising Cody, the guard unlocked the door and pulled it open. Matt said, "Come on out here and let's take a walk, Cody."

Matt waited impatiently for Cody to leave his cell and then led him out of the cellblock to a small windowless room. Matt motioned Cody to sit in a gray, steel chair against the wall, and stood in front of him with his hands on his hips. "Your move, Cody. Yes or no."

"I guess it's pretty much black and white for you, Matt, but the way I see it I lose no matter what I do. I just don't see what the hell I gain by helping you."

"Your call, Cody, but I think you're just making another stupid decision. At least if you agree to become a CI you have a shot at not spending a long damn time in prison."

Cody sighed in resignation, "Yeah, and if I do that I'm probably going to get taken out by a drug dealer. If I do nothing, I'll be dead before I even get to trial."

"What the hell does that mean?" Matt asked.

"The word on the cell block is that some folks in here are going to take me out. You remember Tiny, the guy that beat the crap out of me in my cell?" Matt nodded his understanding. "Well, it seems Tiny has quite a few friends in here who do what he tells them to do. Now, Tiny is still pissed at me over what happened to him when he was using me for a punching bag. The fact is, if I stay in here much longer the best that will happen is that I'll get beat up pretty bad. I've heard that there's actually a pool – the person who is closest on the day and time that someone sticks a shiv in me takes the pot. And the heavy betting is on this weekend."

Matt couldn't help smiling, "That's good to know, Cody. I think I'll take Sunday at noon. Where do I get in on the action?"

"Not funny, Matt. So, I guess the answer to your question is that yes, I'm ready to be a CI. But I'll only do it if you can get me the hell out of here before the weekend. If you can't, no deal."

Matt considered that and said, "That may be tough, Cody. We need the DA to go to a judge and get him to let you out. The problem is that right now the DA is really wound up about a double murder that happened yesterday. I don't know if I can get him to focus on this. But I'll try. At least for now we've got you in a cell by yourself – if you're smart you'll take your meals in here and not leave the cell for any reason. I'll get back to you when I have something."

NINE

Law Offices of Elliot Z. Finkleman, Esq.
5:30 P.M.

Elliot Finkleman sat behind a battered desk in a small, disheveled office that reeked of moldy files and stale cigarette smoke. To his left, a small metal table was littered with old files from long-closed cases and a carton containing a half-eaten Chinese dinner from last week. To his right, a gray steel bookcase contained several outdated criminal law treatises and more haphazardly stacked old files. Aside from a small light fixture overhead, the only illumination came from a small window that provided a partial view of Liberty Street. Elliot glanced at the window and it vaguely registered that the streetlights had flickered on, marking for him another meaningless day that had now faded into a meaningless past.

The forty-five years that Elliot had spent on this earth had taken a heavy toll, and that showed in his physical appearance. He was a small man, standing about five foot, five inches tall with a wiry frame and a badly stooped posture. His pale complexion was highlighted by a full, but unkempt, black beard, and his bloodshot brown eyes blinked incessantly. What most people first noticed about Elliot, however, was that he radiated a sense of sadness.

The office was closed for the day, not that it really mattered since paying clients were few and far between. Reluctantly, Elliot opened a letter from his landlord which, as he expected, threatened eviction if his past due rent was not paid within ten days. He tossed that letter on top of a stack of other unpaid bills, and sighed as he reached into the lower drawer of his desk and removed a bottle of Old Crow Kentucky Bourbon. That beverage was once famous for its quality – it had been the favorite of Ulysses S. Grant and Mark Twain – but long ago the recipe had changed for the worse, and it was now the drink of choice for those who could afford no better choice. Elliot poured two inches into a clouded glass that hadn't been cleaned in recent memory and took a healthy swallow. As soon as his throat stopped burning from the first drink, he drained what remained in one gulp. Elliot put the glass on his desk and turned to close his desk drawer, but hesitated as his eyes focused on a couple of small, waxed bags that bore the Ace of Diamonds stamp.

Elliot sensed that he was about to cross a dangerous threshold but no longer gave a damn. The bags were given to him several days earlier in partial payment of his fee; each of the bags contained a dose of heroin. He knew that his "alternative" fee arrangement could get him permanently disbarred, but since the client lacked the resources to pay in cash and the bags had some street value, he took them without further thought. Although Elliot had smoked marijuana regularly since college, and over the past few years had taken to using Vicodin when he could afford it, he had always considered heroin to be in a different and dangerous category, a line that he wasn't ready to cross.

Elliot closed the drawer and then reached for the bottle and refilled his glass as he reflected on the fact that his had been a pathetic, misspent life. It had been nearly twenty years since he graduated from the University of Pittsburgh Law School, and he could still remember what it felt like to look ahead to a future bright with promise. He began his career as a prosecutor with the Allegheny County District Attorney's office, where he quickly progressed from prosecuting misdemeanors to major felony cases. Elliot seemed to be on the fast track until he publicly characterized the District Attorney's handling of a high profile case as "incompetent" and "bordering on malpractice," thereby ended his career as a prosecutor. After that, Elliot managed to catch on with a small criminal defense firm, but once again found himself unwelcome when during a firm meeting he called the managing partner an "obnoxious little jerk with a room temperature IQ." Having burned his bridges in the Pittsburgh criminal law community, he decided on a whim to move to Franklin, the seat of the Venango County courthouse, and establish a solo law practice.

Elliot's plan was to survive on court-appointed criminal cases until he could establish a more flourishing practice with higher-paying private clients. That plan was sadly misguided. Plainly, there were more than enough criminal defendants in the area to support a thriving practice. Yet, Elliot was a socially awkward man who simply could not attract a steady stream of clients nor win the respect of his peers. In his rare good times, he represented a parade of sociopaths whose creativity in violating the laws of the Commonwealth of Pennsylvania was both impressive and highly disturbing. Most often, he sat in his office reading the newspaper and hoping that a client would walk through the door, or in a courtroom hoping that a judge would take pity on him and appoint him to represent some miscreant who did not have the resources to pay for his own defense.

As he thought about it, he realized that it all came down to this: Elliot hated the practice of law, the miserable clients and the obnoxious attorneys whom he had to deal with, but he didn't have any realistic alternatives. Each morning when he awoke, the thought of going to his office for another mean-ingless and empty day made him nauseous, and with each passing week he sunk further into depression. The breaking point occurred yesterday, when he learned that his girlfriend had been sleeping with one of the Venango District Court judges. *The Goddamned bitch. The whole three years that we were together she was screwing the judge on the side.* He threw his glass at the wall, where it shattered against his framed law school diploma and knocked it to the floor.

Slowly, as if it were Pandora's box, Elliot opened the desk drawer. After a moment's indecision he removed the wax bags and a brown paper bag from the drawer and placed them on the desk in front of him. He closed his eyes and concentrated on the instructions that his client had given him, and when he had it straight in his mind opened the paper bag and pulled out a hypodermic needle and some cotton. *I may as well go all in and shoot up since it'll give me twice the high that way. I can't afford to waste this stuff.* Elliot wrapped a rubber band around his arm, found a protruding vein and cleaned it with an alcohol swab. The client hadn't actually mentioned that step, but that's what they did in the doctor's office. He opened a bottle of water and used the needle to withdraw about 50 units of water, which he squirted into a plastic spoon. He couldn't recall how much of the heroin powder he was supposed to use, so he put two packets into the spoon and mixed it with the plunger from the syringe. Next, he added a small piece of cotton to act as a filter. He put the needle into the cotton and pulled the plunger back, drawing the mixture into the needle.

As he held the needle, Elliot was gripped by fear. *This is really dumb, Elliot, what the hell are you getting yourself into? You have no idea what's in those bags and how it will affect you.* He put the needle down and tried to make sense of it all, but the overwhelming thought going through his mind was that he had failed at everything he had tried, so what the hell did he have to lose? After about five minutes of indecision he picked up the needle with a shaky hand, slid it into a vein and slowly pressed the plunger.

As the Ace of Diamonds – heroin mixed with a substantial amount of far more powerful fentanyl – entered his system Elliot felt an immediate sense of euphoria, unlike anything he had ever experienced. The next thing that he knew his head was on the desk – he had passed out and then regained consciousness. He was surprised that the high was even greater after he passed out. The euphoria was followed by a severe bout of nausea, which soiled his desk and everything on it. He looked at the needle still sticking in his arm and thought that he better remove it, but he felt an overwhelming sense of drowsiness and then passed out again. Had he been conscious, Elliot would have realized that his breathing had become very shallow and his heartbeat had become irregular. As the drug began to overwhelm his body Elliot started foaming at the mouth. After a few minutes his heart stopped beating and he finally achieved the peace that had eluded him for so many years.

No one would find Elliot until ten days later when the landlord finally lost patience with his failure to pay his rent and came with a locksmith to change the locks to his office.

TEN

Pittsburgh
10 P.M.

Gus Amoroso settled into his favorite chair with a glass of Vin Santo. He picked up a cantuccini, a traditional Tuscan almond biscotti, dipped it in the Vin Santo and savored it while he admired the view of the Pittsburgh skyline from the living room window of his thirtieth-floor penthouse. After finishing the cantuccini, he reached for the remote control and turned on the television just in time to catch the start of the 10 O'clock news. The reporter standing in front of the distinctive Venango County courthouse caught his attention, and he turned the volume up as the anchor announced:

> "As part of our ongoing investigation of the opioid crisis in the Franklin area, Channel 5 reported earlier today that a jogger found the bodies of two males dead of gunshot wounds on the banks of the Allegheny River in Franklin. We've just learned that one of the victims was handcuffed with police-style handcuffs, and the second victim died of gunshot wounds to the head. TV5 reporter Mercedes Boone brings us this

update live from the Venango County courthouse."

"Thanks, Bill. Here's what we've learned so far. In a bizarre and gruesome double murder, a jogger found two bodies on the riverbank here in Franklin. We don't have the identities of the victims yet, but we're told that they're twenty- to thirty-year old white males. Our exclusive confidential source tells us that one of the victims died of injuries inflicted by a point-blank shotgun blast. The second victim was killed by two 9-millimeter shots to the head. And here's where it gets really bizarre – police have recovered the 9 mm pistol used in that shooting, and our source tells us that the only fingerprints found on the weapon belong to Franklin Police Chief Robert Miller."

The video shifted to file video of Chief Miller walking into the Franklin Police Department.

"We understand that Chief Miller has taken administrative leave and that the Venango County DA is investigating. We've been unable to reach the DA for comment, but the speculation within the Department is that the Chief may be charged with first-degree murder. A spokesman for the Franklin PD declined to make any public comment, citing the ongoing investigation. None of the sources that we've talked to could come up with a plausible motive, but at this point all signs point to Chief Miller as the principal suspect. One of our sources speculated that

Chief Miller might even be tied to an incident earlier in the week in which a woman was shot to death and a man seriously wounded in a deserted parking lot in Franklin. The TV5 news team is continuing its investigation and will report further news as its breaks. Back to you, Bill."

Gus spilled his wine as he leapt out of his chair. "Driver, you crazy son of a bitch, how in the hell did you pull that off?"

From the bedroom, a plaintive, impatient voice called out, "Turn off the TV and come to bed, Gus, you know I have to be home first thing in the morning before Walter gets back. We don't have any time to waste." Margaret Kelliher, the Franklin Mayor's athletic, thirty-year old redheaded wife, came in to the living room wearing nothing but a smile and the new diamond necklace that Gus had given her earlier that day. "Unless you'd really rather watch the news."

SECTION IV
OPENING MOVES

ONE

Matt's Cabin
Friday, December 22
2 P.M.

Matt was sitting on his patio in front of a roaring fire pit, drinking a cold Straub's beer and struggling to understand yesterday's events. Although he refused to believe that the Chief was guilty of murder, undeniably his gun and handcuffs had been used to commit the crime. He stood up, stirred the fire and angrily threw a stone into the river. *If he didn't kill those people, someone must have set him up. But how the hell did they do that?*

Matt had bought the cabin several months earlier at a foreclosure sale, and was renovating it in his spare time. Although the cabin was his dream home – a secluded spot in the woods on the river – he had been reluctant to buy it out of concern that the prior owner, a VHI manager who had been laid off and could no longer make the mortgage payments, would lose his home. But Matt finally decided that that someone was going to buy the cabin, and it might as well be him.

Normally, Matt treasured the tranquility of the woods and could easily lose himself in his work on the cabin, but today his concerns enveloped him like a wet blanket. He had planned to start installing the hardwood floor in the great room later today, but just couldn't work up the enthusiasm for that. Not even the thought that Erin, his girlfriend of six months, was driving in from Ohio tonight to join him for a three-day weekend could brighten his mood.

As he grabbed another log from the woodpile, Matt thought that he heard the sound of a car coming down the dirt road towards the cabin. He paused and listened, but the sound was gone. *Must be my imagination. There shouldn't be anyone driving down that road.* Matt tossed a large log on the fire, causing a stream of sparks to erupt into the air. He settled comfortably into his chair, and then considered starting on the new floor. He quickly rejected that idea, retrieved another Straub's from the kitchen and settled back into his chair by the fire pit.

He thought he heard a faint rustling sound in the woods and listened carefully, but the noise was gone. *Probably just a deer. I really do need some time off. I'm wound up so tight that I'm hearing things.*

Matt propped his feet up on the stones surrounding the fire pit and began to plan his weekend. He had gotten as far as mentally undressing Erin the moment she came through the door when the warmth and gentle crackling of the fire caused him to nod off. The mostly empty beer can slipped from his hand and spilled its remaining contents on the ground. Matt slept contentedly for an hour, until the fire gradually died down and the blanket of warmth that it provided dissipated. He slowly awakened as he began to shiver in the afternoon chill, and then stood to stretch out the kinks that had developed in his muscles from sleeping in the chair.

Matt tossed a couple of new logs on the fire and went into the house to make a cup of coffee. As he did so, he heard a distinct creak caused by someone stepping on one of the old floorboards in the cabin. *That's not my imagination. There's someone in the goddamned cabin. Damn it, my pistol is locked in the gun safe in the bedroom. This is not good.* Matt looked around for something that he could use as a weapon, grabbed a crow bar that he had left on the ground earlier and quietly circled to the front of the house. He distinctly remembered leaving the front door closed and locked, and yet the door was now ajar. His pulse was now racing as he considered who might be waiting for him inside and what his next move should be.

Matt carefully pushed the front door open enough to peek inside; there was no one visible and nothing obviously out of order. He silently opened the door enough to slip into the cabin. Directly ahead he could see that all was secure in the kitchen. To the right, the great room was empty and harbored no threats. He next looked to the left and saw that the bedroom door, that he always left open, was closed.

OK, someone – maybe more than one person – is in the bedroom. I don't know why they're in there and whether they're armed. I could go back outside and try to look in the bedroom window, but they'd probably either hear me going back out or see me standing outside. The only weapon I have is a crow bar, and that isn't going to help me very much if I'm facing a gun. On the other hand, I have the element of surprise on my side.

Matt considered his options and decided that he would kick the door open and deal with whoever was in the bedroom. After pausing for 30 seconds to listen for any noises that might give him a clue as to what he was facing, Matt slowly and silently approached the door and raised the crow-bar so that he was ready to strike and prepared to launch himself through the door.

Before he could move, the door opened and he heard a shrill scream. Matt dropped the crowbar and stood paralyzed in front of the door.

"That's a hell of a way to greet a girl, Matt." Erin was standing in the door wearing a sheer negligée and a thoroughly pissed off look. "You scared the crap out of me."

After standing speechless for a moment, Matt finally stuttered, "I, I, ah, thought you were, um, an intruder."

Erin's anger quickly faded as she saw the humor in the situation, "You get half-naked women breaking into your cabin very often, Matt?"

They both collapsed in laughter. "Damn, Erin, I'm so happy to see you but I thought you were coming in later. I heard a noise in the house and thought someone had broken in. Why didn't you let me know you were here?"

"I was trying to surprise you. And it looks like I did! I parked the car up the road and snuck down through the woods. When I didn't see you in the cabin I looked out back and saw you sound asleep in front of the fire pit. So, I thought I'd let you sleep and go change into something that might catch your attention when you woke up."

Matt broke into a wide grin. Slowly and obviously he dropped his gaze from her violet eyes, visually caressed the pert breasts that were straining against her negligee and then settled on her black pubic hairs. "Well, you sure have my attention. What shall we do now?"

Erin reached for Matt's belt and unbuckled it, unzipped him and let his pants fall to the floor. Matt kicked off his pants, picked Erin up in his arms and carried her into the bedroom and gently laid her on the bed. Matt and Erin spent the afternoon making love and finally fell asleep in each other's arms.

A hundred yards away, in a well-concealed spot in the woods, Driver calmly put down his binoculars and chuckled. *I hope you enjoyed that, Riley. I'll deal with you soon enough.*

TWO

Cuernavaca, Mexico
2:20 P.M.

El Animal, puffing angrily on a large black cigar, paced slowly across his private office. He was not a man accustomed to waiting for others, and Arturo Cardenas was twenty minutes late. His temper had slowly reached the boiling point. Five minutes earlier, Rema had silently slipped out of the room when she realized that she would be the sole target for his violence. She had once before made the mistake of remaining in his presence during one of his temper tantrums and did not wish to repeat the experience.

Cardenas, one of his principal lieutenants, had called an hour earlier and insisted that they meet right away. El Animal had tried to put him off, arguing that surely they could discuss the matter over their encrypted phones or meet in person the next morning, but Cardenas bluntly refused. After threatening to have Cardenas' balls cut off and fed to him, El Animal finally relented and changed his plans for the afternoon so that they could meet. Now, he found himself standing around waiting like some peón for Cardenas to show up. El Animal removed a pistol from his desk drawer and tucked it into the front of his waistband, then kicked a trashcan across the room, scattering its contents wildly. Just as the trashcan came to a rest against a wall, Cardenas entered the room.

"Where the fuck have you been, Cardenas? Do you think I have nothing better to do than wait for you all afternoon?"

Cardenas, a former Colonel in the Cuerpo de Fuerzas Especiales, was not intimidated. He calmly walked across the office to a cabinet where El Animal kept his best scotch and poured himself a glass. He raised the bottle questioningly to El Animal, who indicated with an icy nod that he would have a glass. Cardenas set both glasses on a small conference table and took a seat.

"Before we talk, perhaps you should put the pistol away before you accidentally shoot yourself in the nuts. That would be very painful, and your girlfriend would be very disappointed."

El Animal glared at him briefly before deciding that no offense was intended, then laughed and replaced the pistol in his desk drawer.

Cardenas continued, "My apologies for being late, Jefe, but I needed to get information that I knew you would want. You will understand when I explain what has happened."

El Animal sat down and picked up his glass, and then said in a menacing voice, "Cardenas, just what is so damned important that we couldn't discuss it over our encrypted phones?"

Cardenas swirled the scotch in his glass for a minute and said, "Over the past two days several of our shipments through Reynosa have been intercepted by the state police. At first I thought that this was simply bad luck, our people perhaps being too obvious and making it difficult for the police to look the other way. But I now know that is not the case.

You are asking yourself, no doubt, how did this happen when we have paid important people so well to prevent this? That is why I am late; I was seeking answers to this question. The answer, sadly, is that we have been betrayed."

Surprising Cardenas, who expected an angry outburst, El Animal calmly but icily said, "Tell me what happened."

"As you know, we have paid the Governor and the local head of the federales much money to allow our drugs to pass through Reynosa and cross the Rio Grande. The deal was that the state police would seize an occasional small shipment, so that it looked like they were doing their job, but leave our major shipments alone. The loss of some drugs and an occasional courier was just a cost of doing business." El Animal nodded his understanding and waited for Cardenas to continue.

"This worked well until last week. Our people have been able to move freely – you remember that in 2013 the Reynosa police were disbanded after the Cartel killed half of them. We paid off the governor, the heads of the state police and the federales. Given the choice of dying in a futile cause or becoming wealthy, they took the money. So, the only danger was the federales on the American side. We have a bounty of $20,000 for each American border patrol agent, dead or alive, and several of the agents are on our payroll. While we have lost some drugs at the crossing, the loss level has been acceptable."

El Animal was growing impatient again. "Arturo, why are you wasting my time telling me things that I already know?"

Cardenas ignored the interruption and continued, "This afternoon I learned that the governor has ordered the state police to intercept our shipments and arrest our people. I was late today because I wanted to be sure that what I am about to tell you is fact, and not just a rumor. Last night the state police arrested the head of our Tamaulipas operations at a roadblock. He was not brought to the jail, and his body was later found in a ditch with a bullet in the back of his head. That was a message to us. In addition, over the last couple of days, several of our large shipments – more than fifty kilograms – have been seized in Reynosa. Because of those losses, we are unable to meet all of our commitments."

El Animal locked eyes with Cardenas and said, "Do you have any more bad news for me, or are you ready to tell me what we should do?"

"That is all of the bad news. And here is my suggestion as to what we should do. Ever since the new governor of Tamaulipas was elected in 2016 we have had problems. Before, we had strong ties to the Institutional Revolutionary Party, and their politicians kept things under control. Of course, the Americans were unhappy, and they even indicted the two previous IRP governors on drug charges – as if the Americans run things in Mexico! But since the IRP lost power, our politicians have been less reliable, and now this new governor has openly defied us. He is even planning to hold a conference in Reynosa on ending the drug trade. We must send a message that this will not be tolerated."

El Animal screamed, "Who the fuck do they think they are? We make them rich and this is how they repay us? Enough! Kill them both immediately. And make sure that you do it in a way that will make it clear that we will not tolerate traitors."

Cardenas laughed and said, "I thought that you would

say that, and the plans are in place waiting for your approval. If you will excuse me for just a minute." Cardenas picked up his cell phone, pushed several keys and waited for an answer. "Execute plan Reynosa." He put the phone back in his pocket, picked up his scotch and said to El Animal, "Our problem will be solved within 72 hours."

THREE

Mayor's Office
4 P.M.

Warren Holmgren arrived precisely on time for his appointment with Mayor Kelliher. Holmgren was a tall, dark-haired, athletic-looking 45-year-old man who had spent his entire career with Venango Heavy Industries – "VHI" as it was known to the locals. Last year he had been promoted to general manager of the Franklin plant, the city's largest employer. Holmgren was intensely proud of that achievement, and viewed the people who worked at the plant as his extended family.

VHI had maintained its headquarters in Franklin for over fifty years, along with a large industrial complex that produced massive coal mining machines. As environmental restrictions gradually strangled the coal industry, however, the demand for the machinery needed to produce coal slackened. With that decline came a series of layoffs, the impact of which rippled through the local economy.

Holmgren was having a difficult time controlling his anger as the secretary showed him into the mayor's office. On a personal level, he detested the mayor, whom he considered an incompetent and selfish little weasel who always put his own interests above all else. But what really angered him was the message that he was bearing for the mayor.

Two days ago, Holmgren had received an unexpected phone call from the Chairman and Chief Executive Officer of VHI. "Holmgren, I'm afraid I have some bad news for you. As you know, we've been working with McGuiness Partners, the Boston-based consulting firm, to analyze our operations with a view to maximizing our efficiencies and increasing shareholder value. Well, they've completed their analysis, and it comes down to this: the Franklin plant is underperforming, and there's no way that we can afford to make the sort of capital improvements necessary to bring the plant up to snuff and still achieve the return on investment that our shareholders expect. So, we've made the decision to close the plant as of March 30 of next year."

Holmgren stuttered, "But, but, but, there, well, there must be something we can do. My people depend on this plant… I could talk with the union about some additional concessions, and maybe get some tax relief from the city. I've been looking into both of those things recently and they're promising but I need some time . . ."

The CEO cut him off before he could complete the thought. "It's a done deal, period. So save your breath. A bunch of Harvard PhDs who are a lot smarter than you and I ran their computer models, and numbers don't lie."

Holmgren shot back angrily, "This is about real people, dammit, not just a bunch of numbers cranked out by a bunch of academics that probably don't even know what the inside of a plant looks like."

"Listen very carefully to me, Warren. I had planned to

find another place in the company for you, but if I hear one more word out of you other than 'yes sir' I'll terminate you today."

The CEO paused briefly, heard nothing but silence, and then continued. "Now, there's a whole bunch of legal BS that we have to go through to close the plant and get all of those damned people off of our payroll. Our labor relations staff will deal with the unions on this. They're going to be really pissed, and I wouldn't be surprised if the unions stirred up some violence at the plant. Someone from Legal will call you later today and walk you through what you need to do. I need you to meet with the Franklin mayor on Friday afternoon at 4 PM. We're going to roll this out to everyone at the same time, so I don't care how you do it, just make sure that you get an appointment with the mayor at 4 PM on Friday. Once this news gets outside the company, it will travel fast. For Chrissakes, don't tell anyone else until then."

Holmgren started to argue with his CEO but he heard a click and the line went dead. He stared at the phone wordlessly for a minute and then let the handset fall to the floor as he slumped back in his chair.

"Come on in, Warren, and grab a seat. What's so important that you had to see me this afternoon? I really don't appreciate you calling and demanding a meeting time. I'm not one of your flunkies."

"Yes, Mayor, it is important." He handed an envelope to Kelliher, who looked at it curiously. "I've been directed by my CEO to give this notice to you. I'm sure that you'll want to read it carefully, but the bottom line is that the Venango Heavy Industries Franklin plant will close permanently as of

March 30. All of the employees will be laid off as of that date. I understand that the plant will be demolished on April 7."

Mayor Kelliher exploded, "You can't do that! That plant is the only major employer left in this town. If you do that, it will kill any chance for me to get re-elected."

Holmgren exploded, "You miserable little shit. Over 200 people are about to lose their livelihood and your only concern is how it will affect your re-election? I'll tell you something. There's nothing that I, or anyone, else can do to save that plant. That ship has sailed. But I'll damn sure do everything that I can do to make sure that you do not get reelected. This town deserves better than the likes of you."

Holmgren stood up and walked out of the office, ignoring Kelliher's screaming, "Damn you, you can't talk to me that way. I'm the Mayor of this town. You'll pay for this!"

FOUR

Venango County Jail
6 P.M.

Cody was laying on his bunk wondering how he was going to get out of the mess he was in when he heard rapid footsteps moving down the corridor towards his cell. Cody sat up and turned toward the front of the cell in time to see one of the guards stop in front of the door.

The guard unlocked the door and said to Cody in a loud, hostile voice, "Get up, Ware, apparently someone has bailed your miserable ass out of jail. Not that you'll be out long before you screw up and end up back here. Come with me." The guard glared impatiently at Cody, and waited for him to get out of bed and walk to the cell door. "Move your goddamned ass, I don't have all day."

When Cody reached the cell door, the guard grabbed him roughly by the arm and propelled him towards the jail's administrative area. *What the hell is going on here? This has to be a screw-up, no one is going to post bail for me. I'm not sure that anyone even knows that I'm in here.* Cody started to turn and ask what was happening when he noticed Matt standing in the hallway. The guard let go of Cody's arm when they reached Matt and walked off. Matt gave him a look that signaled that he should keep his mouth shut, and pushed Cody though the jail and out the rear door onto Otter Street. As they walked out the door, Cody turned to Matt.

"Just what the hell is going on, Matt?"

"Sorry about the rough treatment, Cody. I told the guard to make a scene so that everyone would hear that you're getting out on bail and that the cops are pissed off about it. We don't want people wondering why you just disappeared from jail and speculating about what happened. Anyway, you wanted out tonight; you're out. So, we're going to walk across the street to the courthouse and you're going to talk with the DA. We've got your street clothes and your personal stuff over there. When we're done, you can go home. No one is going to pick you up on the prior warrant."

Dennis Archer opened a door and brusquely walked into the small, private conference room that adjoined his office. Lieutenant Tucker and Matt Riley, both in uniform, were seated at a small wooden table that occupied much of the room. Between them, still wearing his prison uniform, sat Cody Ware. Archer sat down, and in a harsh, even voice began the meeting.

"I don't like this CI idea one damn bit, but I don't have a better option. Ray, just so we're all on the same page, give us an update on this afternoon's incident on Railroad Street. I'm assuming that Matt and Mr. Ware aren't up to speed?" With a shake of his head Matt indicated that he didn't know what was going on, and Cody's look of confusion confirmed that he was clueless. "So, Ray, start from the beginning."

"OK. Here's what I have. At 3:55 this afternoon we responded to a 911 call at a duplex on Railroad Street. One of the residents authorized my officer to enter the house, and he found four males and two females who were unresponsive. He observed drug paraphernalia and what he believed to be heroin. I'll spare you the details, but the bottom-line is that four were pronounced dead at the scene and the other two died at the hospital."

Matt and Cody exchanged concerned looks. This new piece of information made Cody's CI role more important – and more dangerous. Lieutenant Tucker continued.

"Now, here's where it gets really bad. We don't have the lab results yet, but I think what we have is something called "Ace of Diamonds," which is heroin cut with fentanyl. This is really powerful stuff, and over the last couple of weeks it's shown up in several nearby communities and caused multiple fatalities. It's here in Franklin now, and we're going to have more fatalities if we don't stop it."

Archer glared at Cody for a full 30 seconds before speaking. "Just so that you understand where I'm coming from, I think you're a miserable, smart-mouthed little jerk who ought to rot in prison. And it really pisses me off to give you a break. But we need to find out who is moving this Ace of Diamonds into Franklin and stop them right now. Lieutenant Tucker tells me that you can help us there, and Matt tells me that we can trust you. I highly doubt that, but I'm going to take a chance." Archer paused to take a drink from the water glass on his desk. While he did that, Cody shifted uncomfortably in his chair and looked between Matt and Archer.

"So, here's the deal. You're out of jail right now because I convinced the judge to release you on personal recognizance. The charges have not been dropped, and I can have you thrown back in jail in a heartbeat. Do you understand that?" Cody silently nodded his understanding.

"In return, you will act as a confidential informant. What that means is that you will do *exactly* what Tucker and Riley tell you to do to get inside the local drug ring, identify the leaders and obtain evidence that will lead to their convictions. Once we arrest them, you will be a key witness when I prosecute the bastards, and your testimony will be critical to getting a conviction. One thing that you can count on is that the dealers will get the best defense lawyers that money can buy, and those guys will do everything that they can think of to make you look like the bad guy and their clients look like altar boys."

Archer paused and looked Cody straight in the eye to make sure that he had his full attention. "I think you know that this will be dangerous – if the dealers even suspect that you're a CI, you'll be a dead man. That means that you'll have to keep your cool when you're working with them even though you may be put into some pretty hairy situations. But if you pull it off, I'll drop all of the charges except child endangerment. There is just no way that I can ignore the fact that you took that little girl on a drug buy. But I'll throw you this bone: when you go to trial I will tell the judge that you cooperated with us at great personal risk, and ask for a suspended sentence. In other words, no jail time unless you screw up again. But there are no guarantees – the judge can do what he wants for sentencing no matter what I recommend."

Archer looked at Lieutenant Tucker and made a gesture asking if Tucker had anything to add. Tucker thought for a second and shook his head no. Archer turned back to Cody.

"If that is acceptable to you, I'm going to have you sign a written agreement. What I want to make sure that you understand is that you will be authorized to do certain specified things that would otherwise be illegal, such as drug transactions. If you do anything illegal *beyond* what we authorize you to do, you will be arrested. If you engage in any violence, other than in self-defense, or use any drugs, you will be arrested. If you lie to us, you will be arrested. The only thing that I want to hear from you is that you understand this deal and are willing to go along with it."

Cody looked directly at Archer. "Yeah, I hear you and I'll do it on your terms. I don't see that I have much choice. We both know that I won't survive in prison. But to be honest, I've been doing a lot of thinking lately – you have a lot of time for that when you're sitting in a jail cell – and I can see that I've fucked my life up pretty bad. I'm not making excuses, but I've had a lot of help along the way – from the doctors that hooked me on painkillers in the first place to the dealers that reeled me in. So, you're looking at me like I'm the problem, but I think you have it wrong. No one sets out to be an addict. No one wants to live like this. And if you really want to fix the problem, you're going to have to do more than arrest a bunch of dealers."

One by one Cody made eye contact with each of the people in the room to make sure that they understood his point, then continued. "So, I'll help you. But here's what I want to be sure that *you* understand. I don't want to be hung out to dry – if I finger a dealer and testify in court, I want to be sure that you're going to burn them, and burn them bad. I don't want to hear that some politician made you back off, or that you don't think the evidence is quite strong enough for a conviction so you're going to let them cop to a plea. No bail, no probation, no minimum sentence. I read the papers, and I know that you guys let a dealer walk a couple of weeks ago. I want to be sure that you're all in – you're going to go for convictions and max sentences. Are we agreed?"

Archer stared at Cody in disbelief. "What the hell, you're calling *my* hand? Jesus, that's a new one. Yeah, Ware, I can guarantee you that I'll go all out if we get these people. Lieutenant Tucker has a form for you to sign that covers the terms of our agreement, and he brought your street clothes over from the jail so that you can change out of that jail uniform. You'll deal with him and Matt from here on out, I don't want to see you or hear from you under any circumstances." Archer stood up and walked out of the conference room.

FIVE

Red Dog Lounge
7 P.M.

Cody was apprehensive as he walked into the Red Dog Lounge, a small bar on Liberty Street a few blocks from the courthouse. *Great*, Cody thought, *my first move as a CI is to meet a cop in public. I am so fucking dead.* He paused to allow his eyes to adjust from the nighttime darkness to the relative brightness of the bar, and his first impressions were the smell of stale cigarette smoke and beer, and the sound of loud, twangy country and western music. Cody hated country and western music, the Pennsylvania rednecks that listened to it and the tricked-out pickup trucks that they drove around town.

The Red Dog was about half-full, with most of the thirty or so patrons watching the Penguins hockey game showing on the two large-screen televisions hung over the bar. Although the TV sound was turned down so that others could listen to the music, a loud cheer erupted as the Pens scored a short-handed goal to take a 1 – 0 lead. Despite Cody's fears, no one paid any attention to him. His next thought was, *country and western music and ice hockey; I must have already died and gone to hell.*

Cody scanned the bar and quickly spotted Matt in a dark

corner, wearing jeans and a plaid wool shirt instead of the police uniform that he had worn an hour earlier. As he approached the table, Matt motioned for him to sit down. The two men looked at each other awkwardly for a moment, neither fully trusting the other but realizing that they needed to reach an understanding. Matt drained his beer glass and said. "Well, Cody, you look a lot more comfortable in street clothes instead of a jail uniform. Loosen up, no one will recognize you in here, it's not your type of crowd. What'll you have to drink?"

"How about a soda?" When he saw the confused look on Matt's face Cody explained, "I can't drink, Matt. That's how it starts for me. First it's a beer, then I'm back on drugs. I've been through rehab three times, and the relapse always starts with a beer. Even though I know that I shouldn't touch the stuff, it's hard to say no when you're hanging out with people and everyone else is drinking."

The waitress came over and Matt ordered another Straub for himself and a soda for Cody. When she left, Matt said, "Time for us to have a serious talk. It's pretty noisy here, and folks are watching the game, so if you keep your voice down we won't be overheard. If we're going to work together I need to know what you're thinking. So, truth time – why did you agree to be a CI?"

"I guess there's a couple of reasons. One, I don't really have a choice and you know it. I'm just picking the least bad of my two options and hoping to survive it. Two, and you probably won't believe this, I thought that maybe I could do something positive for a change. I've seen a hell of a lot more than you about how drugs – and I don't just mean heroin – are screwing up people's lives. I had a good friend overdose last month; I was there when it happened and it scared the crap out of me. He just died, right in front of me, and there wasn't a damn thing I could do about it. Until then, I heard about people dying from an overdose but I knew that it wouldn't happen to me, right? Suddenly, it became very real. It finally hit me that life is precious and we're all just one bad decision away from it being over. I was about to say, you don't know what it's like to see a friend die in front of you, but I guess that's not true, is it?"

Matt nodded sadly, "Been down that road too many times. Same thing, we all thought we were bullet proof. You think that something bad might happen to the other guy, but not to me. The day I got shot, I was trying to rescue one of my squad mates. I knew that it was going to be a little hairy, and I might even get dinged. But no big deal, right? Well, I watched the guy get his brains blown out while I was holding him, and then I took a couple of rounds that tore me up pretty bad. So, yeah, I know what you're talking about."

Cody continued, "Hmm, I never thought about it that way, but I guess we all cope by pretending the bad stuff only happens to the other guy."

Matt took another sip of beer and agreed, "In Afghanistan, if we didn't think that way we couldn't make it through the day. Every time we left the compound people would shoot at us or there'd be an IED explosion. You had to convince yourself that everything would be OK or else you couldn't function."

There was a short silence as both were lost to their thoughts. Matt broke the silence, "Cody, explain something to me. How did you get into drugs? I heard you say that no one chooses to be an addict, but I'm pretty sure no one held you down and forced it on you."

"I guess that's a fair question. It's a little different for everyone, I think, but I can tell you what happened to me. Maybe that will help you understand the problem. I don't know if you remember this, but I had a pretty bad car wreck when I was a junior in high school."

Matt shrugged, indicating that he didn't recall the wreck.

Cody continued, "I was working at the Pegasus restaurant – you know the place, right?" Matt nodded affirmatively. "I got off work at eleven one Saturday night. It was snowing, but it didn't seem too bad, and I hadn't been drinking or anything. At that point I'd never had hard liquor or drugs. Anyway, when I hit the brakes coming into the curve at the bottom of the 15th street hill, the damn car didn't slow down. It just slid head-on into a beer truck. I knew as soon as we crashed that I was hurt pretty bad. At the hospital, the doctors told me that the crash had broken my collarbone, a couple of ribs and my right arm, and they had to sew up a pretty good gash on my forehead. I was in a lot of pain, so they put me on Oxycodone."

Matt replied, "Yeah, I know what you mean. After I was shot in Afghanistan, they put me on something like that for a while."

Cody said, "That's right, I heard that you did some sort of Joe Hero thing and got shot up pretty badly. I guess we have that in common. Well, not the hero part, just the prescription painkiller part. Anyway, the Oxycodone really helped with the pain, but it also gave me a good high that made all of my problems go away. After a while, the doctors said I had healed up OK physically and didn't need it anymore. Oh, but I did.

I craved it, and couldn't get through the day without it. The bottom line is that I got hooked on dope because they started me on prescription pills after the accident."

Matt asked, "But, if they took you off of it how did you get the pills?"

"Come on, Matt. You're a cop. You know that stuff is everywhere. In Third Ward, someone in about every fifth house is dealing – usually small-time stuff by people trying to pay for their own habit. On the off chance that you don't know someone who's dealing, or at least dealing what you want, you just take a ride down the street and watch for someone oddly hovering near a stop sign. That's the runner. Now, he'd spot you as a cop in a second – you just look like one, OK? But if you're cool and you pull up and ask him what he's selling he'll set you up. I thought you cops knew all this stuff."

"Maybe so, but I'll bet you can fill in some blanks for me."

"OK, so let's back up to what happened to me. At first, I managed to buy Oxycodone on the street - it's not that hard to find, really. You'd be amazed at the number of people who get some pill mill to prescribe Oxycodone and have Medicaid pay for it, keep some for themselves and sell the rest on the street. It's a good way to supplement their income, right? And you know that the drug gangs send people to various doctors to get prescriptions so that they can sell them on the street?"

Matt took a long pull from his beer and said, "Yeah, we're trying to crack down on that by using a computer data base to track prescriptions. That way we can identify doctors who are writing way too many prescriptions."

"Good luck with that one," Cody replied cynically. "The gangs will figure out ways to work around that. Hey, did you ever hear about Dr. Feelgood?"

Matt laughed, "Yeah, I remember that. The feds busted him right after I joined the force. What was his real name . . . that's right, Doctor Richard Pelosi. Everyone called him Dr. Feelgood, because if you could manage to walk into his office and say ouch, he'd prescribe Oxycodone. I heard that he wrote the most Oxycodone prescriptions in Pennsylvania for five years straight. When they busted him, they found out that the sonofabitch had stacks of pre-signed prescriptions for Oxycodone so that his staff could just hand them out without even bothering the doctor.

Cody said, "Yep, that's the guy. What ever happened to him, anyway?"

"Well, the way they finally caught him is that he started supplying Oxycodone to a 17-year-old girl in return for sex and her mother found out. The mother went ballistic, and that's when it all started to unravel. He got 15 years in the federal pen."

Cody nodded, "Well, I guess we won't be seeing him for a while, but there's others doing the same thing. Anyway, getting back to how I got hooked, I did pills for a while, but that's kinda pricey. About $1 a milligram, and I needed a couple of 60 mg pills to get high. And then one day, my dealer gave me a little heroin to try, and didn't even charge me for it. Kind of a loss leader, I guess. And, you know what, that was a lot cheaper and gave me a better high than the prescription pills. Of course, the longer I was on heroin, the more I needed to get a high and the more it was costing me."

Matt thought about that, and said. "The thing I really don't get is how you can stick yourself with a needle."

Cody looked down at the table and thought deeply for a minute before replying. "For a while I didn't get that either. I always thought that people who did that were disgusting. For the first three months I just snorted it. But, the more I got drawn in, the less judgment I seemed to have. Once day my girlfriend dumped me, and I was depressed and just didn't give a damn. A friend told me that if I shot up I could get twice the high for half the dope, and I thought 'what have I got to lose?' So, he showed me how to do it right in the men's room of the Franklin Library. Once you get over the weirdness of shooting up, it's no big deal."

Matt looked as if he was going to say something, but changed his mind. Cody and Matt sat for a moment, looking away from each other, in an uncomfortable silence. Finally, Cody continued.

"But, that's just how I got into it. A lot of guys do it because they are so fucking depressed about living in a dying town with no real jobs, no future and not a hell of a lot to do. You have no idea how much that gets to you, Matt. They start out on a little weed and then maybe move to Vicodin. After a while they figure out that heroin is cheaper and gives a better high, so they move up the food chain, so to speak."

Matt guzzled the last of his beer, belched, and held the bottle up to signal the waitress that he needed a refill. Then, he turned back to Cody and said, "Where I have a hard time following you is, I was on opioids after I was wounded – hell, the medics fired me up with fentanyl right after I was hit – and I never felt the need to get high after they weaned me off of it. I'll grant you, some of the people in the military hospitals with me did the same thing as you, but I always figured that they were trying to escape from something."

Cody shook his head. "Nah, it ain't that simple. It's in your blood, man. Some people – I'm one of them – just get addicted to the stuff. If it wasn't heroin, I'd probably be an alcoholic. I think it runs in the family; I have an uncle who's an alcoholic and one of my grandparents was too. Other people – I guess you're one of them – don't seem to be affected as much. Don't get pissed at me, man, but I think part of it is that you've always been one of those guys who follow *all* of the rules. They tell you drugs are bad, so good little Matt wouldn't think of doing drugs. Have you ever broken a rule in your whole fucking life, Matt? You should try it sometime – it makes life a lot more interesting."

"I've been around the block a few times, Cody, so don't hand me that shit. You're missing my point; all it takes is a little self-discipline. You saw what happens to people who do heroin, and yet you went down that path. It didn't just happen, you made a choice."

Cody snorted, "I figured you'd say something like that. Maybe that's how it works in your world, but not in mine. It's easy for you. You were the big stud in high school, and then you managed to escape Franklin. You know, I really envied you when I heard about that. Next thing I hear is that the Marines gave you some sort of fancy medal for being a hotshot just before they booted your ass out the door. So, then I thought maybe there's just no escaping this place."

Cody sipped his drink, and continued, "Then you come back here, and the next thing you know, you've landed a job with the cops – nice salary, nice benefits, what's not to like? And if that isn't enough, you're hooked up with some college hottie. Try living your life when your choices are working at a convenience store for minimum wage or going on welfare, and the only women in your dating pool have at least three kids, each by a different father."

"Oh, bullshit Cody. You're trying to tell me that it's not your fault, you're a product of your environment? Cut me a break, I'm not buying that crap. Even if I did, my pity isn't going to get you anything. Your life is what you make it. You make decisions, and those decisions have consequences. That's why you ended up in jail bunking with a guy named Tiny. How about taking some responsibility for your own damned life?"

Cody glared at Matt, "You want me to help you, and I'm trying. I'm telling you the way it is. You ever wonder why there's a market for heroin? Well, it ain't because people wake up in the morning and decide they want to be a junkie. It's despair, man. You really don't understand that feeling of hopelessness, do you? You just need an escape. I hate dope so fucking much because I love it so fucking much. I know it's eating me up, but most of the time I just don't give a damn. And why should I? That's what you're fighting, Matt. As long as people like me need an escape from their meaningless, fucked up lives, there will be demand. And as long as there's money to be made, there will be dealers."

"So what, we just give up and watch people waste away?"

Cody sighed in frustration, and his voice rose. "I'm not saying that, dammit. You think that if you can lock up enough people that will fix everything? Not in the real world, Matt. You're just pissing in the wind. All that happens when you arrest a dealer is that a new one steps in. There's just too much money involved." Cody paused for a minute to collect his thoughts. "Well, maybe arresting dealers helps some, but you gotta fix the despair. You arrest addicts and throw them in jail, treat them like a piece of shit. You don't have enough room in all of the jails to hold them. And even when you do bust them, as soon as they get out they start using again – so what's the point? You need to fix the problem, man. Give folks some hope. Look around you, Matt. What the hell is there to do in this town?"

"OK, Cody, you win. Let me get my magic wand and I'll fix everything. Seriously, how the hell do you fix despair? Sure, we need to fix some things here in town. The Franklin economy is shot, and I don't see it coming back. No one seems to want to step up to the plate around here to try to fix things."

"Yeah, ain't that a bitch. All the politicians care about is collecting their paychecks and getting reelected. But, even if they could do something to fix the economy and give people some hope, they still need to do something to help people who *do* get addicted." Cody saw the dubious look on Matt's face and a note of frustration entered his voice. "People screw up, Matt. Stop acting like you think it's all their fault. Once you get hooked on drugs like heroin it's really hard to go straight. So, where do you turn for that? There are a few groups around here that have counselors, but if you want to have a chance you need to go to a rehab center, and that's expensive. You know, I've OD'd three times already – the second time almost killed me because I tried speed balling."

Matt's look made it clear that he didn't know exactly what Cody was talking about.

"Seriously, you don't know that speed balling means shooting up with a mixture of heroin and cocaine? You get the heroin high and the cocaine energy – it makes you feel like Superman. But you have to have a death wish to do it because it's hard to get the dose right, and if you take too much it's deadly. Anyway, I've done rehab three times, but I'm just like most people – I stay straight a couple of months and then something bad happens and you relapse."

Matt's patience with listening to things that he neither fully understood nor accepted had reached its limit. "So now we're back to you need someone to hold your hand to keep you from stubbing your toe? That's bullshit. I know a little something about despair. When I was shot, it wasn't the physical pain that got to me. It was the fact that what I really wanted to do in life was suddenly taken away from me. Being a Marine was who I was, and I didn't have a clue as to what I would do with the rest of my life. So I came back here to be with my family, and at first all I did was sit on my ass collecting a retirement check and moping about what I had lost. I finally got it together, but it wasn't because someone held my hand and told me what to do."

Cody snickered at that, "Now you're the one who's laying down the bullshit. The way I heard it, you were so depressed when you got back that you almost never left your father's house. And I'll bet that you drank your share of booze back then, right?"

"So, I tossed a few drinks back, what's the big deal?" *A few drinks my ass, I killed half a bottle of scotch most nights. But drugs are different.*

"Sure, a few drinks, we'll go with that. So, what made you crawl back out of the bottle?"

Matt wasn't sure if it was Cody's attitude, or that his remark hit too close to home, but he desperately wanted to punch Cody in the mouth. *You little prick, who the hell are you to question me? I could rip you in half without breaking a sweat.* He calmed down after a few seconds and said, "My family pushed me pretty hard to back off the sauce, and after a while I just got sick of laying around all day feeling sorry for myself. *And a really good ass-chewing by Chief Miller pointed me in the right direction.* But, to answer your question, it wasn't until I signed on with the Franklin PD that I really got it under control."

Cody was seeing a new side of Matt. "So, you needed a little help to get through it?"

Matt took another pull from his beer, "I guess I didn't want to admit that to myself. Yeah, I was going down a bad road for a while. It wasn't just that I was out of the Corps, there were some things going on in my head. Some of the things that I saw – well, you can't unsee them. I still have nightmares about it, Cody. Human beings – savages, really – at their absolute fucking worst. And, at times, at their absolute best." Matt's face showed that he suddenly realized that he had pulled back a curtain on his soul for the first time, and just as quickly his expression changed and the curtain closed. "Aw, hell, it don't mean nothin."

Cody saw the change in Matt's expression, and he realized that something still deeply troubled Matt. He also realized that now wasn't the time to probe. "I guess we have to play the cards that we're dealt. But one thing that I think I've figured out over the last few days is that it ain't OK to take chances with other people's lives."

It was obvious to Cody that Matt didn't get his point. "Let me try to explain what I mean. Before I do, is this between us?

I'm not going to hear you testifying about it in court?"

"Sure, why not? You've got my word on that."

"OK. The thing that's been bothering me over the last couple of days is that little girl you told me about who accidentally OD'd because her mother left stuff out. She had no idea that she was being exposed to something that could kill her. That really hit home because me and Brandi really tried to be careful not to leave anything out where Daisy could reach it, but there were times where we were so high that we did. We were just lucky that nothing like that ever happened to Daisy."

Matt scowled and his voice hardened, "I find that hard to square that with you bringing Daisy on a drug buy. And don't feed me your line about just doing a U-turn in the parking lot."

"Look, I get it, that was dumb and I'm not going to try to excuse it. But what you need to understand is that when you're on heroin, the only thing you care about is your next fix. You'll steal your parents or your girlfriend blind to make your next score, and I know that because I've done both. Judgment goes out the window. I'm not saying it's right, I'm just telling you the way it is."

Matt looked thoughtful. "I hear what you're saying, Cody, I just don't know what to think about it. I'm not even sure how we ended up going down this path. Let's get back to the details of how you're going to work with me as a CI."

It only took Cody and Matt five minutes to go over the ground rules and work out procedures for communicating with each other. When they were done, Cody stood up and walked out of the bar. Matt paid the tab, and was deeply troubled by their discussion as he headed for his car.

SIX

Saturday, December 23
7:45 A.M.

Matt slowly awakened as the sunshine began to filter through the cabin window. Erin was asleep on his shoulder, and he silently watched her chest slowly rise and fall with the gentle rhythm of her breathing. He smiled as that sight warmed his heart, and then suddenly froze as the reality of what had happened last night dawned on him.

Not long after they had drifted off to sleep for the first time, Erin was awakened by Matt thrashing and moaning in his sleep. Erin tried to calm him by putting her hand on his chest, and realized that he was soaked with sweat. Just then, Matt let out a terrifying scream, "Noooo! Campbell! No!"

Erin was scared and confused. She tried to gently shake him awake, but when she did he grabbed her arm with terrifying strength, threw her on her back and jumped on top of her. She was crying and trying to cover her face to protect against the blows that she was sure were coming when Matt started to come out of it.

"Oh my God, Erin? What's happening?" Erin, sobbing hysterically, tried to speak but Matt couldn't understand a word that she was saying. He tried to pull her close to comfort her, but she pushed him away and retreated to the side of the bed and continued sobbing.

Matt was confused about what had happened and sat quietly on his side of the bed. Finally, Erin calmed down enough to say, "You hurt me Matt. I'm really scared. What's going on?"

"I'm sorry, Erin, the nightmares came back. I don't know what triggers it. I've always been alone when it happened."

"What nightmares?"

"It's a long story, and you probably don't want to hear about it. That was another life."

"I may not want to hear about it, Matt, but I need to hear about it. I have to understand what just happened."

Matt stared at the ceiling, visibly deciding whether he would answer Erin's question.

"Goddamn it, talk to me, Matt!"

"OK. You know I was wounded in Afghanistan, right?"

Erin nodded quietly. She had seen the scars on his body from the bullet wounds and the subsequent surgeries, but sensed that he didn't want to talk about it so never asked. Now, for both of their sakes, she needed to understand what he was going through.

"I still have nightmares about that day. I don't know what sets it off, but it seems to happen a couple of times a month. It's so vivid. It's like I'm reliving it all over again, all of the same sights and sounds, even the smells of the battle. It's almost worse, in a way, because you know what's coming but you can't do a damn thing to change it. I usually wake up in a pool of sweat, and I'm exhausted. But I've always been alone when it happened. But, when I woke up this time I was on top of you and you were crying. What did I do?"

"You were screaming something about 'Campbell,' so I tried to wake you up. When I touched you, you threw me on my back and I thought you were going to hit me. Your face was contorted in rage. It was really scary."

"I'm so sorry, Erin. When you're in that environment you're on edge, jumpy. People are trying to kill you, and it's weird because one minute everything is calm and suddenly all hell breaks loose. I guess you startled me and that set me off."

Erin processed that for a minute, and then decided to explore that later after she understood more about what had happened. She looked Matt straight in the eye and asked, "Who was Campbell?"

Matt's chest started to heave and he broke into tears. "Campbell was a guy in my squad that I was trying to save the day that I got hit. He was down on the other side of a canal, and we could tell that he was hurt bad. So, I went after him and tried to drag him back to our side of the canal. We almost made it."

For a minute that felt like eternity Matt starred silently into the darkness, his hands fidgeting nervously. Finally, he regained his composure and continued. "I've never talked about this before with anyone. We almost fucking made it. Can you understand that? We were so close, all we had to do was climb out of that filthy canal and take cover. But before I could lift him out of the canal there was a horrible sound - I'll never forget it – and his head just exploded. I was still holding on to him, but what I was looking at wasn't Campbell anymore, it was a grotesque lump of bloody meat. His brains and blood were splattered all over me. I remember shouting

'No! Campbell!' and then everything went black. That's when I was hit."

Erin moved across the bed and held Matt tightly. "It's going to be OK, Matt. It was just a bad dream. It'll be OK."

"It wasn't just a dream, it really happened. And now it keeps happening over and over in my head. Maybe if I had done something differently Campbell would be alive today."

"I know, honey, but it's behind you now. We can work through this. Have you seen anyone about the dreams?"

Matt stiffened. "You mean, like a shrink? Hell no. I'm not crazy."

"I know you're not. It'll be OK." Erin knew that Matt would need some professional help to get through this, but that this was not the time to push that subject. She continued to hold Matt and talk soothingly with him. Gradually, Matt calmed down and eventually they fell asleep in each other's arms.

When morning broke, and as he waited for Erin to awaken, Matt's mind was in turmoil. Tonight, Erin would meet his family for the first time. It was a longstanding family tradition that everyone would gather at his father's house for Christmas Eve dinner, and he wanted the evening to be special for everyone. Yesterday, he had visited Feldman's Jewelers and, after much agonizing over his choices, picked out an engagement ring. He had planned to ask for her hand as soon as everyone was seated for dinner.

Now, everything had changed. After she experienced his nightmares and his violent reaction, would she still feel the same about him? He didn't think that he would ever hurt her, but how could they know for sure?

SECTION V
GAME ON

ONE

The Southern Airways Express commuter flight from Pittsburgh dropped violently as it descended through a heavy cloud cover on its path to the Venango County Regional airport. When the flight left Pittsburgh, the weather had been overcast but not particularly threatening. That changed about mid-way through the 25-minute flight when the plane encountered a storm front, and with it a heavy, sustained turbulence.

Shortly after the turbulence began, Pete Broggi, the sole passenger on the 9-passenger Cessna Caravan aircraft, seized his armrests in a death grip and turned a pallid white color. While Pete didn't exactly fear flying, it could fairly be said that he was *very* apprehensive whenever he flew. He particularly disliked smaller aircraft, and the Cessna was the smallest plane on which he had ever flown. Even at his modest 5 foot 9 inch height, when he walked in the aisle he had to crouch so that his head didn't hit the ceiling.

During the flight, the cockpit remained open, with not even a curtain separating it from the passenger compartment.

Pete took little comfort from the fact that the two pilots were laughing and seemed wholly unconcerned by the turbulence. *Those guys don't look old enough to shave, let alone fly an airplane. Holy Christ, I just realized that the copilot is the same guy that took my ticket and carried my bag to the plane. They'd probably have no clue if the wings were about to fall off of this thing. Dear Lord, if you let me survive this I promise I'll start going to church again.*

With a lurch, accompanied by groaning metallic sounds, the Cessna dropped several hundred feet and broke out of the clouds. Soon, Pete saw that the plane was lined up with the runway and he released his grip on the armrest just long enough to grab a handkerchief and mop the sweat from his forehead. *My God, that runway is way too short for this plane to land on, and there's snow starting to accumulate. Hail Mary, full of grace, blessed be thy name. . .* Pete felt a solid jolt as the plane impacted the runway, and was thrown against his seat belt as the pilot reversed the propeller pitch sharply and quickly slowed the plane to a stop. With a sigh of relief, Pete took the empty airsickness bag from his lap, replaced it in the seatback pocket and mopped the sweat from his forehead one last time.

The pilot shut down the engine and turned to Pete, "Hang on for a minute and they'll have the door open. I hope you enjoyed the flight." *Sure, almost as much as a trip to the dentist. My God, is that guy even 18?* The ground crew opened the passenger door, and Pete arose shakily from his seat, thankful for the burst of cold, fresh air. He cautiously descended the steep ladder to the tarmac and waited briefly for the crewman to retrieve his bag from the baggage compartment. Pete casually took the bag and walked to the terminal, giving no hint that the bag contained anything more than business papers or perhaps a change of underwear. In fact, it contained two kilos of heroin that had been slipped inside by a ground crewman in Pittsburgh who had been paid handsomely for his efforts.

Pete had flown to Franklin because the debacle with MF confirmed that it was time for a change in Franklin. He was pretty happy with his role as one of several mid-level people in Gus' organization, and, if he didn't clean up the Franklin mess, some very important people would conclude that Pete was part of the problem. The organization wasn't like a company where HR called you in and said, "sorry, your performance review was below average. You need some remedial training." No, people who dropped the ball tended to drop out of sight - permanently.

As he was walking to the terminal Pete mused over the fact that there was a surprisingly robust market for heroin in these small towns. *Pretty damned weird. You wouldn't think there'd be a lot of demand in a poor area like this. Hell, half the addicts are getting welfare and juicing that up by stealing anything that isn't nailed down, but they find a way to come up with the cash. You gotta love this business. It's just like having your own personal ATM machine.*

Pete followed the ground crewman into the small, concrete block terminal and looked around. The terminal consisted of a single check-in counter, restrooms and a restaurant named Primo Barone's. There were only two other people in the terminal, one an obese gray-haired woman wearing an ill-fitting floral dress who looked to be in her early sixties. Pete walked past her and approached a twenty-something Hispanic man with an arrogant demeanor who was leaning casually against the wall. Pete carefully examined the man who, by process of elimination, must be his contact. *This is the guy who we're going to set up as our Franklin distributor? None too bright looking, and he's sure not going to intimidate anyone.*

"Are you Nick?"

The man slid his sunglasses down on his nose and glowered at Pete for a moment before saying, "Who's asking?"

Pete tried to stare him down, but failed.

"You retarded or just deaf? I said, who's asking."

Pete bristled at being insulted by the smart-assed little punk, but responded, "I'm here to meet Nick." Pete made a mental note to arrange for an attitude adjustment for the punk, but not until he had new arrangements firmly in place in Franklin.

The man now had considerable menace in his voice as his hand slipped into his jacket pocket, "Last chance, asshole. Who's asking?"

"Pete Broggi. What's with the attitude?"

The man nodded toward the restaurant. "Black-haired guy with sunglasses sitting at the table closest to the door."

Pete continued to stare at the man until he relaxed and removed his hand from his pocket, then Pete turned and walked to the restaurant. There was only one customer, who occupied a table set for two near the door. Pete walked to the table and asked, "Nick?"

"Yeah, and you're Pete, right?"

Pete sat down without being asked. "Yeah. So, what's with the little spic with the bad attitude?"

Nick frowned at that insult, and responded with an edge to his voice, "I always like a little insurance."

"Well, he's little, for sure, but I don't think he's much insurance."

"Looks can be deceiving." Nick fixed Pete with a hard stare for a moment, and then his look softened. "How was your flight?"

"Oh, no big deal. We had a little turbulence, but no sweat." *Well, it's a miracle that I didn't lose my lunch, but I'm not about to tell you that.*

"Great, I was afraid it might have been rough coming in. One of your pilots walked straight to the bar over there and ordered a double scotch – I hope he's done flying for the day – and I heard him tell the bartender that the last 10 minutes were a real bitch." Nick chuckled, "It was the younger one, probably the copilot, and he said that it was the worst that he had ever seen. I got the feeling that in a few more minutes he and his lunch may have parted ways."

Before Pete could respond, a middle-aged waitress, who looked like she had been there as long as the restaurant, approached the table. "Here you go, two cheeseburgers, medium well, and two diet sodas. Will there be anything else?"

Nick thanked the waitress and turned to Pete, "I hope you don't mind. I don't want to be here too long, and everyone likes a good cheeseburger, right?"

Pete's stomach rumbled as he looked at the burger, but he looked at Nick and said, "Sure, why not. Let's get down to it." Both men surreptitiously looked around to make sure that their conversation wouldn't be overheard, and leaned closer to each other across the table so that they could talk softly.

"This will be our only meeting, and we have a few things to discuss. You know that our previous associate here in Franklin has become *unavailable*." Pete paused and stared directly at Nick to underscore the fact that Tony and MF had become 'unavailable' because they had crossed the wrong people. When he was sure that Nick understood the point he said, "We want you to pick up his business."

Nick took a bite of the cheeseburger, talking while he chewed, "Yeah, Tony and his guys were in over their heads. I think you'll find my people are more professional. Shit, shooting that girl was really dumb. So, how are you going to get the product to me?" He idly wiped the morsels of hamburger from his chin.

Pete slid his bag to Nick under the table. "What was agreed upon to get you started. You have something for me?"

The surprised look on Nick's face signaled his realization that Pete had carried the drugs with him on the plane, and just as quickly his expression changed as he realized that Pete had people in place to make sure that he would not be caught. *Impressive, these guys are well connected and know what they're doing. This arrangement could be very interesting.* Nick slid an envelope across the table. "It's all there. So, how did you get the package through airport security? Wasn't that pretty risky?"

Pete's condescending tone suggested that he thought this was a dumb question. "It was magic Nick. I just said the magic words, and there it was." In fact, Pete didn't know how the drugs were brought into the Pittsburgh airport. Unbeknownst to him, Driver had made arrangements to pay $5,000 per shipment to a mechanic who had a badge that permitted him to bypass the usual TSA security checkpoints. The mechanic would place the Ace of Diamonds in a sports bag filled with clothing and carry it through the employee entrance to the terminal. Once inside the terminal, the mechanic would go to a coffee shop near the gate for the Franklin flight, where he would sit next to the courier and place the bag between them. Although normally a low-level courier would take the drugs from the mechanic and carry them to various destinations – they had done this almost forty times so far without incident – Pete decided to take them himself today since he was traveling to Franklin.

Nick didn't care for Pete's condescending attitude but decided to let it pass. This could be a very good business relationship for him, and he didn't see any sense in screwing it up over something trivial. He took another large bite of the burger and washed it down with soda. "So, how are we going to do business in the future?"

Pete tucked the envelope into his pocket without looking at it and looked Nick straight in the eye. "First off, what's left of Tony's old gang will be pretty pissed when they find out that you're taking over. My people will pass the word that we won't look kindly on any violence that will increase police interest in our operations. That should be sufficient. What I need from you is an understanding that if there's a problem you'll let us handle it and not get into a turf battle."

Nick considered that and nodded, "Done, so long as your people really handle it. It shouldn't be a big deal because most of Tony's people – the good ones at least – are working for me now. But if one of my people gets whacked, all bets are off."

"Fair enough. As far as moving the merchandise, we'll

use different routes each time, and we'll let you know a day ahead when and where the drop will be. We'll use this route sometimes, but usually we'll just have a courier drive it in. Same quantity, same price for now, then we'll see how things go. Think of it as a probationary period."

Nick bristled at the mention of a probationary period. "That probationary shit works both ways. I'm gonna grow the business, and I need a reliable supplier. If you can't do it, I'll make other arrangements. So, who's going to be bringing the stuff in?"

Pete struggled to maintain his temper, but gave no outward sign that he was angry. *You really don't get it, hotshot. There are no other suppliers. You cross us and you're dead.* Pete forced himself to smile and said, "We'll use different couriers. You'll get the meet place and the time by text. If our courier senses something wrong he'll take a pass and we'll text you the new arrangements."

"OK. Your guys will be dealing with Eduardo, my 'insurance policy' that you met earlier. He's waiting outside and can drive you into town if you'd like. That would give the two of you a chance to work out some details."

Pete took a drink of his soda, and then spoke in a quiet, menacing tone, "Nick, I've had enough of that little prick for a lifetime. I thought it was understood that when I came here today that I would meet with you and nobody else. I don't want anyone else in your organization to know who the fuck I am. Are we clear on that?"

Nick stuffed the remainder of his burger into his mouth, "Yeah, I hear you. I didn't get that word, but it ain't real healthy for people in our profession to walk around here without an insurance policy. But I'll have a word with Eduardo; you were never here. Anything else?"

Pete stood up. "That's it. You know how to get in touch if there are problems. And, I have to add, I don't want to hear about any problems." Pete walked out of the restaurant and headed for the parking lot.

TWO

Reynosa, Tamaulipas State, Mexico
2 P.M.

**United States Department of State Level 4
"Do Not Travel" advisory for the Mexican state
of Tamaulipas:**
*Do not travel due to crime. Violent crime, such as
murder, armed robbery, carjacking, kidnapping, ex-
tortion, and sexual assault, is common. Gang activity,
including gun battles, is widespread. Armed criminal
groups target public and private passenger buses
traveling through Tamaulipas, often taking passen-
gers hostage and demanding ransom payments. Local law enforcement has limited capability to respond
to violence in many parts of the state.*

Reynosa, Mexico, and McAllen, Texas, are separated only
by a narrow stretch of the Rio Grande River and some
worthless scrubland, and yet the two cities are worlds apart.
Reynosa bears the twin distinctions of being one of the largest Mexican border cities, with a population of approximately
600,000 people, and also one of the most dangerous. The city
exists in a state of near-anarchy, captive to the whims of drug

cartels that enforce their control through unspeakable brutality and whose running gun battles in the city's streets are the norm rather than the exception.

Drug-related violence in Reynosa exploded in 2010 when Los Zetas, which had been formed with deserters from the Mexican Special Forces to serve as the enforcement wing of the Gulf Cartel, split off from its parent. That triggered a wave of violence as various gang leaders, and would-be leaders, fought for control. From 2010 through 2015 there were more than 15,000 murders, giving Reynosa a higher per capita death rate than the Iraq and Afghanistan war zones. After years of cartel warfare, Reynosa's streets are lined by bullet-pockmarked buildings and burned out vehicles.

In Reynosa, a seemingly mundane decision, such as choosing a route to work in the morning, can be a matter of life or death. Competing gangs roam the city with impunity, setting up roadblocks to ambush their rivals, and innocent bystanders are often caught in the crossfire. The local authorities dare not interfere, but in a weirdly practical accommodation the City of Reynosa issues "red alerts" which provide the location of ongoing gun battles to help residents plan their daily commute. After all, drug wars or not, life must go on.

In contrast, while McAllen, Texas, is one of America's poorest cities, it nevertheless remains governed by the rule of law. McAllen features sights not markedly different from other Southwestern cities, with palm tree lined streets and familiar chain stores and fast food joints spread as far as the eye can see. Its residents go about their daily business for the most part undisturbed, and drug violence is generally something that they watch on the local TV news while shaking their heads and deploring the senseless violence on the other side of the border. While inexorably some of the Reynosa violence has spilled across the border, McAllen remains safe enough to attract so-called "snowbirds" – retired residents of northern states – during the winter months.

Despite their differences, Reynosa and McAllen have two common bonds. The first is the legitimate cross-border flow of commerce, where goods from Reynosa "maquiladora" factories, as well as from elsewhere in Mexico, flow into the United States through McAllen, and conversely American goods flow south through Reynosa. The maquiladora factories employ more than 100,000 people in Reynosa alone, explaining in large part why people continue to live in a city so plagued by violence. The second bond is that the stretch of river dividing Reynosa and McAllen is one of the major pathways into the United States for illegal drugs. Just as the legitimate commerce is fueled by demand for consumer goods, the drug trade is fueled by an insatiable American demand for substances such as heroin and fentanyl.

The Reynosa – McAllen drug pathway had been controlled by the Gulf Cartel and the Zetas, but their constant warfare had left both groups splintered and weakened, a virtual invitation for others to stake their claims to this path. A year earlier, El Animal had decided that the time was right for GDM to become the major player on this path and he acted decisively. Ironically, El Animal succeeded by adopting the Zeta's tactic of overwhelming brutality: early one morning the local leaders of three competing gangs and the mayor of Reynosa were found hanging from an overpass leading to the McAllen – Hidalgo – Reynosa International Bridge.

Each of the four men had been mutilated, and each bore a sign around their neck with a warning written in their blood: "GDM does not forgive or forget." From that day forward, no one interfered with GDM shipments through Reynosa.

Now, however, a new crop of politicians vowed to end the drug violence and make Reynosa once again a livable city, and the government had suddenly grown bolder. Both the Army and the national police had implemented an aggressive program of random roadblocks throughout the city to intercept gang members and disrupt their business, and the authorities focused particularly on the GDM. Not only had several shipments been seized, but also seven GDM members had been killed during the government crackdown.

El Animal was willing to tolerate only so much, and today there would be a reckoning. Over the past several days, nearly one hundred GDM fighters armed with automatic weapons, rockets and hand grenades had quietly gathered in two widely separated locations on the outskirts of Reynosa. One group set up near the Aeropeurto General Lucio Blanco, and a second gathered to the west of the city. Both groups took great pains to conceal their presence. At 4 PM the two groups, each forming a convoy protected by heavily armored vehicles, simultaneously began moving towards their assigned targets.

The first clash occurred at 4:30 P.M., when a GDM convoy heading toward the central city unexpectedly encountered a Mexican Army roadblock on Calle Revolución. The roadblock consisted of two armored vehicles blocking the intersection, supported by a squad of soldiers. After two uneventful days, the soldiers had become lax and inattentive; that would cost them their lives. In contrast, the GDM fighters knew that they were heading into battle and were alert with their weapons at the ready.

As soon as the GDM column turned onto Calle Revolución, they saw the roadblock and immediately attacked. The lead vehicle skidded to a stop, two men exited and took aim with AT4 anti-tank weapons that El Animal had obtained at great cost on the international arms market. The 84-mm HEDP (High Explosive Dual Purpose) rounds penetrated the armored vehicles and exploded, destroying the vehicles and showering the soldiers with shrapnel. Simultaneously, GDM fighters in a second vehicle opened fire with their pedestal-mounted 50-caliber machine guns and sprayed the roadblock with hundreds of rounds. Before the soldiers could bring a single weapon to bear, all of them were dead and their burning vehicles marked the sky with columns of acrid smoke. The battle occurred so quickly and violently that not a single GDM fighter was wounded.

As the lead GDM vehicle skirted the shattered army vehicles and continued toward the target, its driver coldly surveyed the collateral damage that their firepower had caused. Several civilian cars were burning along the side of the road, and the flames had spread to several buildings. Further down the road, he saw a mother clutching her daughter and leaning against the passenger side of a parked car behind which she had sought shelter. Scores of GDM machine gun rounds missed their target and penetrated the car, tearing into the bodies of the mother and her child. As the convoy passed, the mother stared at it with sightless eyes and the child's screams grew faint and finally stopped as her lifeblood drained away. The driver, unmoved by the sight, ran over the corpses of several other innocent bystanders and continued to his target.

Two minutes later the convoy stopped at the Gran Reynosa hotel, where the mayor and the Tamaulipas governor were holding a press conference on their plan to eliminate drug violence in Reynosa. The GDM fighters stormed the hotel and burst into its large conference room. The plan worked perfectly, as two international TV news crews filmed the bodyguards dying in a futile attempt to protect the mayor and the governor, and numerous bystanders being cut down in the hail of gunfire. The mayor and the governor were spared, briefly, until the GDM fighters could drag them outside, behead them and hang their heads from lampposts in front of the hotel. To underscore the message, a sign beneath the severed heads proclaimed, "GDM does not forgive or forget."

Five miles away, the second GDM column reached its target at roughly the same time that the mayor and governor were being executed. This target was the commander of the National Police in Reynosa. El Animal's sources had learned that he would be visiting his mistress in the apartment that he kept for her in the eastern side of the city. The GDM forces quickly eliminated the commander's protective detail and broke down the door to the apartment. A burst of automatic weapons fire killed the police commander and his mistress. Because there were no press cameras to record the event, the GDM fighters simply tossed a sign on the bed, "GDM does not forgive or forget."

The two columns quickly dispersed before the Mexican authorities could react. That evening, El Animal smiled as he watched news reports on the carnage. He was confident that there would be no further attempts to interrupt his business.

THREE

Franklin City Hall
5 P.M.

It had been a long day, and Mayor Walter Kelliher decided that he deserved a peaceful snort in the privacy of his office before going home to face his wife. *The damned woman will start nagging me about God knows what the second I walk in the door, and won't let up until I agree to whatever silly thing she wants from me.* He pulled a bottle of Glenlivet Archive 21-year-old single malt scotch from his credenza, poured two inches into his glass and followed that with a splash of water.

Kelliher had never tasted scotch before he joined the Ford dealership five years earlier. The owner, a wealthy and pompous man, kept a bottle of Glenlivet 21 in his office and occasionally shared a drink with a salesman who had had a particularly good month. Only once in five years had he been invited for a drink, but he often watched in envy as others were rewarded. Now that he was Mayor, he had his own bottle of Glenlivet conspicuously displayed in his office, and he could have a nip any damned time he pleased. *No more being treated like a goddamned dog that gets a treat for performing a trick,* Kelliher thought bitterly, *'good boy, here's your scotch, now go sell another car.'*

As he sipped the scotch, he put his feet up on the desk and smiled with satisfaction as he opened a five-by-nine-inch manila envelope that had been handed to him that morning as he pulled his car into his reserved parking place. There was no doubt in Kelliher's mind about what was in the envelope. Every month an elegantly dressed man with intense blue eyes and a scar on his face met him in the parking lot and slipped him an envelope containing $20,000. Kelliher slowly counted the $100 bills and grinned. *No more groveling for a lousy drink. I'm pulling down $240,000 a year in tax-free cash that my greedy bitch of a wife doesn't know about, plus the chicken-feed I get for being Mayor. All I have to do is provide a little information to some gangsters in Pittsburgh to help them peddle drugs here in Franklin. They're going to do that whether I help them or not, so what's the big deal?*

Kelliher was in an unusually good mood as he flipped on the TV set in his office to catch the 5 PM news. That reminded him that he had several messages from a TV5 reporter wanting to speak with him. Maybe he'd call her after the news. The longer he could linger in his office, the longer he could avoid the fight with his wife that inevitably would begin the second he walked in the door. The TV flickered on just as the newscast began.

"Our lead story tonight once again is from Franklin, where it appears that there have been multiple drug-related fatalities. Channel 5 reporter Mercedes Boone brings us the story live from Liberty Street in Franklin."

The video switched to a shot of Mercedes standing on Liberty Street, with black and yellow police tape around the scene and a crowd of curious onlookers.

"Thanks, Bill. We have more bad news from Franklin this evening. At about 4 PM the Franklin police responded to a 911 call on Liberty Street. When they arrived, they found six people unresponsive, four males and two females all in their mid- to late-twenties. We understand that a roommate of one of the residents called 911 after he arrived home from work and found several people unconscious."

"The police determined that the individuals had ingested some form of heroin – we understand that it's called the Ace of Diamonds – and proceeded to administer naloxone in an attempt to neutralize the drugs. The EMTs arrived shortly after the police and pronounced four people dead at the scene and transported two others to UPMC Northwest Medical Center in Seneca, where they remain in critical condition."

"A police spokesman was unable to provide the victim's identities or any further details. We've also attempted to contact the Franklin Mayor's office for a statement, but our calls have not been returned. We'll continue to monitor this situation and will provide further details as they become available."

Walter Kelliher gulped down the rest of his drink, grabbed the bottle from his credenza and filled his glass to the brim.

FOUR

Franklin Police Department
11 P.M.

The events of the past several days were still swirling in his mind as Matt began his shift. He was still on a high over the fact that Erin had agreed to marry him. Just before Christmas Eve dinner, while everyone was sitting in front of the fireplace, Matt pulled the ring from his pocket, got down on one knee and proposed; Erin immediately accepted. But, he was deeply troubled by his recent recognition that he was still traumatized by his combat experiences. After much discussion, Erin had convinced him that he had some serious problems that they would need to address together if their marriage was to succeed.

For a change, the weather was mild as he hopped into his patrol car. Without consciously deciding to do so, he headed to Duke's restaurant. That had become something of a routine with Matt, as he enjoyed talking with Heather, a twenty-something waitress that he had come to think of as a little sister.

Matt walked into Duke's and paused briefly when he noticed the one other customer – a chubby woman sporting a blue-tinged Mohawk and a "Make America Great Again" t-shirt – and then sat at the counter. Straight-faced, Matt looked at Heather and said, "So, what's new in your world?"

Heather cracked up laughing and responded, "Not a damn thing new here, Matt, just the same old same old. How about you? I heard a rumor that you were ring-shopping last week, any truth to that?"

"How in the world did you hear that?" Heather just shrugged. "Well, to answer your question, yes I was shopping, and I popped the question on Christmas Eve in front of the family. I guess that would have been embarrassing if she said no, now that I think of it. Anyway, we haven't set a date yet."

Heather slid a steaming cup of coffee to Matt. "Well, congratulations. She's a lucky girl, and I'm happy for you. I hope she's a Penguin's fan!"

"Yes, she is, and better still, she plays center on an intramural girl's hockey team at school. It's kind of embarrassing, but she can out skate me."

"That figures," Heather said, "looks, brains, and a female jock. Sometimes life just ain't fair."

Matt smiled and said, "Yeah, she does have it all. What she sees in me is the part that I don't understand. Anyway, I'll bring her by when I get a chance."

Matt finished his coffee and walked out of the restaurant and to his cruiser. As he settled into the driver's seat, his thoughts were focused on how to sort out what happened to Chief Miller. As he fastened his seatbelt, he noticed some dirt on the console - it looked like a white dust — and idly flicked it away. He shifted the cruiser into gear and headed out on patrol.

Across the street, Driver, sitting in a car parked in a dark portion of a parking lot, removed a surgical mask from his face and pulled rubber gloves off of his hands. He carefully deposited the gloves and mask in a plastic bag and then sealed the bag. Driver stepped out of the car — earlier he had disabled the interior lights so that he wouldn't be seen— and tossed the bag into a dumpster. Confident that he had accomplished his mission, Driver pulled out of the parking lot and headed for his hotel.

A couple of minutes after leaving Duke's Matt's radio sounded, "Unit 7, we have a silent alarm at Feldman's Jewelers on Liberty."

"Unit 7, 10-4, responding." Matt gunned his engine as he reached down and flipped his emergency lights on. He was still a couple of miles away, and decided to leave his siren off to avoid warning anyone who might still be in the jewelry store. Suddenly, he felt a strange tingling sensation in his arms and legs, but dismissed it as unimportant.

Matt began to feel light-headed as he slowed and turned left from 11th Street onto Liberty Street. *That's weird. I must not be getting enough sleep. That was a hell of a weekend.* Matt gunned the engine again as he headed down Liberty. After a couple of blocks his vision started to blur, and he shook his head trying to clear it. Just as he passed the Venango County courthouse, he passed out and slumped forward against the steering wheel. At that point, the road curved left but Matt's cruiser continued forward on a straight line, jumped the curb and hurtled into Fountain Park, where it came to rest against a tree.

Lt. Tucker had heard the Feldman's call and was approaching the store from the opposite direction on Liberty Street when he saw Matt crash. Tucker gunned his engine and reached Matt in less than a minute. Fortunately, Matt's car had been slowed by a clump of bushes before it hit the tree, and the damage appeared to be minimal; the air bag had not even deployed. As he pulled the driver-side door open, Tucker saw that Matt was unconscious. He checked Matt over carefully to see what was wrong, but there was no indication of any injury. Yet, Matt had a very slow pulse and shallow breathing, his lips had an odd bluish tinge and his skin was pale and clammy.

"Oh, shit, it looks like an OD! How in the hell did that happen?" Tucker sprinted back to his car, where he radioed for an ambulance and grabbed two canisters of Narcan. Tucker knew that Matt was a straight-arrow and wondered how he had been exposed.

Tucker ran back to Matt and unfastened his seat belt. As he began to loosen Matt's clothing a large, muscular man in his twenties had emerged from a small crowd that was, despite the late hour, gathering at the scene of the accident. Tucker could hear a low murmur as people asked one another what was happening. "Lieutenant, can I help out?"

In a voice that betrayed his anxiety, Tucker said, "Yes, help me get him out of the car." They laid Matt on the ground, and Tucker injected a dose of Narcan into Matt's thigh muscle. As he finished, Tucker heard the sound of an ambulance approaching in the distance. *Thank God they're quick tonight,* he thought, *Matt is still unresponsive.* "Matt, goddammit, stay with me man. Don't you fucking dare die on me!"

Matt's respiration continued to worsen. Tucker hesitated for a moment, but recalled from his training that multiple doses may be necessary and injected a second dose of Narcan. A minute later the ambulance arrived, its flashing blue and red lights casting odd shadows throughout the park. A paramedic walked up to Tucker, "What have we got, Ray?"

Tucker was relieved to see that the paramedic on duty was Rhoda Mae – she was unflappable and knew her business. "It's Matt Riley. I saw him run off the road and into the park. There's no sign of any injury, but I think he may be an OD. That doesn't make any sense, since he's the last person in the world that would use drugs, and I can't imagine where he might have been exposed. I gave him two doses of Narcan, but he's still not responding."

Rhoda Mae put on gloves and a mask and began to examine Matt. "Aw, crap, we've got a big problem here. He's been exposed to something, probably some kind of opioid, and he's definitely an OD. Get me some more Narcan and the defibrillator from the truck."

While Tucker went to the truck, Rhoda Mae turned to the bystander and asked, "Have you touched the officer or anything inside of the car?"

"Well, ah, sure, the cop asked me to help. So I helped pull him out of the car."

"OK. You stay right there and don't touch anything or anyone. You've probably been exposed to whatever we're dealing with, and I'm going to need to check you out in a minute."

Just then, Tucker returned and handed two containers of Narcan to Rhoda Mae, and she immediately injected Matt while saying, as much to herself as to Tucker, "He's in really bad shape, we could lose him."

While monitoring Matt's vital signs, she turned her head and spoke over her shoulder with an edge to her voice. "Lieutenant,

I thought we trained you people better. You went into that car and handled Matt without gloves and a mask. Whatever the hell this stuff is, you've been exposed. Go sit next to that other guy while I finish here. You may well be my next patient."

Rhoda Mae continued to monitor Matt, and called out to Tucker, "He's still not responding. I'm going to give him another dose, but we need to get him to the hospital ASAP. Lieutenant…. Aw, shit."

Tucker had started walking, but before he was 10 feet away his knees buckled and he passed out, landing heavily on the ground. Rhoda Mae grabbed the other can of Narcan, raced over to Tucker and injected him. She then shifted back to Matt.

Rhoda Mae turned to her driver, who had also donned protective gear, and told him, "Keep an eye on the Lieutenant while I work on Officer Riley." As she checked on Matt, there was a sudden urgency in her voice as she yelled, "Oh, God-damn it, no pulse, he's in cardiac arrest. I'm starting CPR. Get the defib ready."

After performing CPR for a couple of minutes, Rhoda Mae grabbed the defib from her driver and applied the paddles to Matt's chest. The driver went back to Tucker. "OK, the Lieutenant is coming around. I think he's going to be OK. How's Riley doing?"

"Not good. We've got to transport him now. Let's get him on a gurney – I'll need to continue CPR while we transport him to the hospital."

As they were loading Matt into the ambulance, Rhoda Mae screamed at Tucker, who seemed to be stable, and the bystander, who showed no signs of exposure, "Both of you, into the back of ambulance, right now."

FIVE

Mission, Texas
Wednesday, December 27
4 A.M.

Paul Quintze turned his ten-year-old black Chevy pickup truck from the Levee Road into the Rio Club parking lot. He killed the headlights and lowered his window, and then settled comfortably into his seat for what he hoped would be a short wait. At this time of the morning the area appeared deserted. The only light came from a quarter moon that periodically peeked from behind a heavy cloud cover, so Paul donned his night vision goggles and carefully scanned the area. He saw nothing out of the ordinary.

From his vantage point Paul could make out faint glimmers from the river and what appeared to be episodic, stealthy movement of human beings. All that he could hear was the sounds made by nocturnal animals and humans quietly scuttling across the river. From long experience he knew that there would be scores of people crossing illegally from the Mexican to the U.S. side. Just about now, he hoped, someone should be crossing the river with a package for him.

Paul, an unremarkable twenty-year-old man of slender build, had been born and raised in Mission and knew both sides of the river as well as he knew the back of his hand. In his mind's eye, he could see his contact crouched in the low shrubs on the opposite bank, scanning for border patrol agents and any other unwelcome attention that he might attract as he crossed the river. Paul was amused by the fact that, when the man reached the U.S. side and climbed the shallow riverbank, one of the first things that he would encounter would be a fence with a well-lit sign in Spanish pointing the way to a closed but unlocked gate. The fence was intended to keep livestock in, and not illegal immigrants out. After having his fence destroyed several times, the landowner chose the simple expedient of adding a gate and a conspicuous sign asking the immigrants to use the gate, *por favor.* From the landowner's perspective, this tactic had been a great success. The immigration authorities thought otherwise.

Paul preferred to work alone, but this morning he was accompanied by a large, humorless man who was holding an AR-15 assault rifle. Paul knew that the man, who went by the nickname "8-Ball," had on several occasions demonstrated his ability with, and willingness to use, the weapon that he was holding. He was there to safeguard the package that Paul would soon receive. Paul himself was armed with a shotgun, and the two men were prepared to protect the package against all comers.

On the far side of the river, in the town of Reynosa, Miguel Uresti was crouched in the low brush along the riverbank. Beside him was a large plastic cooler that contained 20 kilos of a heroin and fentanyl mixture that, unknown to him, was marketed in the U.S. as "Ace of Diamonds." Miguel didn't give a damn what they called the stuff or what people paid for it. The contents of the cooler, in fact, had a wholesale value of more than $1 million U.S. dollars. After he dropped off the cooler on the other side of the river, he'd return to Mexico.

Miguel was paid handsomely for his role in delivering the Ace of Diamonds into the United States, but he knew that the penalty for losing his cargo would be death. He nervously scanned the area one last time. He was confident that no one would bother him on the Mexican side – the brutal murder of the Tamaulipas governor and the Reynosa Mayor had dampened the appetite of the Mexican authorities to take on the GDM. The American side, however, was an entirely different situation.

As he completed his scan, he noted that there was a lull in the human traffic crossing the river, and no evidence of the American border patrol on the opposite bank. This was as good as it was going to get. To his left, Miguel could see the 130-foot tall steel towers that carried electric power lines across the river, where they connected with the Texas power grid. The power lines would guide him to his destination. Miguel removed his night vision goggles and placed them into a waterproof container. He then tied the plastic cooler to his waist and firmly grasped it as he slid down the shallow riverbank and into the cool, dirty water of the Rio Grande.

Miguel was not prone to deep thought, and he had no clue that he was one small part of a long and complex chain that began in China, where fentanyl in powder form was manufactured and shipped to Mexico. There, the GDM processed the fentanyl and heroin into Ace of Diamonds and arranged to transport it to its various markets in the United States. The drugs that Miguel was carrying this morning were destined for Pittsburgh, where Gus Amoroso's gang would sell them to addicts in several states.

Miguel took five minutes to cross the river, and when he arrived at the American side he crouched in the low brush and again donned his night vision gear and scanned the area for any threats. Satisfied that he was alone, Miguel looked at the electric transmission line tower to get his bearings and then walked to his right along the riverbank until he came to a fence that had a sign pointing him to a gate. *Mierda!* He opened the gate and walked across the property until he came to Levee Road. There, he turned right again and walked several hundred yards to a parking lot, where he saw a black pickup truck with two men in the cab.

Paul was the first to see Miguel approaching the pickup truck, and he nudged 8-Ball and pointed down the road. After seeing what Paul was pointing at, 8-Ball jacked a round into the chamber of his weapon and moved the selector switch from "safe" to "fire." In a pre-arranged signal, Paul flashed a red light twice. In the distance, a red light flashed three times, and then the man began walking to the pickup.

Miguel approached the driver's window, where Paul said "¿Cómo estás, Miguel?"

"Bueno, compadre." Miguel handed the cooler to Paul, who placed it on the console. As he turned back to Miguel to finish their conversation, he saw unexpected headlights come into view on Levee Road. 8-Ball uttered his first words of the evening, "What the fuck?" Miguel muttered, "No Bueno," and crouched behind the pickup. The three men waited to see what the approaching vehicle would do.

Several hundred yards away two high school students were returning home after a night of heavy beer drinking. In their drunken state, they had turned onto Levee Road by mistake. The driver was confused when he saw the sign for the Rio Club. That rang a faint bell in his memory, but he still couldn't quite place where he was. He felt a mild sense of panic because the two would already be in trouble with their parents for being out so late, and wasting more time driving around lost wouldn't help matters. With slightly slurred speech, his friend suggested that they find a place to pull over and figure out where the hell they were.

The driver saw the Rio Club's virtually empty parking lot and at the last minute decided to turn in there so that he could check the map app on his phone and get directions home. This would prove to be the worst, and last, decision of his young life. He braked heavily and turned sharply into the parking lot, causing the tires to squeal in protest. The car overshot the driveway by a couple of feet and thumped across a curbstone before the driver corrected his course and entered the parking lot. The driver said, "Oh crap, my father is really going to kill me if I bent the wheel." The fact that there was a black pickup truck near the parking lot entrance only dimly registered.

Paul and 8-Ball tensed as the vehicle approached. At first, they thought that it would continue harmlessly down Levee Road. They had just begun to relax when the sound of squealing tires signaled that the car – a late model Ford Taurus – had changed direction and was speeding into the parking lot. "Shit, they're coming after us," 8-Ball shouted. When the car jumped the curb, he quickly aimed his rifle and emptied a 30 round magazine into its windshield. The eruption of gunfire prompted Miguel to sprint to the safety of the river and Paul to start his engine. Before Paul could shift the pickup into gear, the car carrying the teenagers had already caught fire.

Paul and 8-Ball watched silently, their ears ringing painfully from the sound of the rifle shots inside the cab, as the car crashed into the side of the Rio Club. Still anticipating return gunfire from the car, 8-Ball inserted a fresh magazine and charged his rifle. There was no sign of life in the car as the flames gradually engulfed it. With a flash of light and a loud whoosh, the car exploded and spread the flames to the Rio Club. Paul looked at 8-Ball, muttered, "Fuck 'em, let's get out of here," and pulled out of the parking lot to begin his journey north.

SIX

Rio Club
6 A.M.

Chief Hinojosa of the Mission, Texas, Police Department was standing in the Rio Club parking lot with his hands on his hips surveying the murder scene. His detectives had combed the area and had found no useful evidence. All that he had was a burned-up car pockmarked by what looked like .556 rounds, the charred bodies of two dead teenagers, a partially burned building and some tire tracks. No witnesses. No shell casings. No reason in the world why these two kids were dead. It just didn't make sense.

As he was surveying the scene hoping to find some clues that he had missed previously, the police beat reporter for the Monitor, the local newspaper, joined him. "Morning, Chief. What the hell happened here?"

Hinojosa shook his head sadly. "Off the record for a minute, Jack?"

"Sure, why not. We can start that way."

"OK. I haven't a goddamned clue. Nothing adds up. Normally I'd say this was a drug deal gone bad. We know they bring stuff across the river down by the power line, and those guys don't screw around. If something looks bad, they just start shooting. But two teenagers? That doesn't add up. I don't know why the hell they were in the parking lot, but my gut tells me they were just in the wrong place at the wrong time. But who the hell killed them and why? I just don't know."

The reporter asked, "Have you ID'd the kids?"

"Yeah, we've got a tentative on them. The bodies were burned beyond recognition, and their IDs were incinerated, but we could read the license plate number. The car was registered to a guy in Mission, and when one of my officers went to his house he confirmed that he let his son borrow the car to meet some friends and that he hadn't come home – he was supposed to be home by midnight. Once he found out what was going on, the poor guy had a meltdown."

"We're still off the record. Who is it?"

Hinojosa said, "Not yet, Jack. We need to ID the other kid and notify the parents. I should have something within the hour."

"What can you give me on the record?"

Hinajosa thought for a minute, and then said, "At about 2 AM two young men were shot to death in the parking lot of the Rio Club. We're still working on identifying the victims, and we don't have any leads on the shooter or the motive. We'd like to talk with anyone who has any information, not that anyone is going to risk their neck by coming forward. That's about all I can give you right now."

The two men stared at each other silently for a minute, shook their heads and walked back to their cars.

SEVEN

UPMC Medical Center
7 A.M.

Dr. Sally Bridges walked into Room 305 and stood at the foot of the bed. "Now how's that for irony? Last week you were handcuffing a patient to the bed in this very room, and now you're the patient. Will we need to restrain you?" Dr. Bridges smiled and put her hand on Matt's hand, "Just kidding. But that is a pretty strange turn of events. So, how are you feeling this morning?"

"A little weak, and my chest hurts like hell. What happened?"

"You know that you blacked out while you were driving down Liberty and ran into a tree at Fountain Park, right?"

"So they tell me. The last thing that I remember was leaving Duke's."

"Well, that doesn't surprise me. The reason that you blacked out is that you were exposed to a drug called carfentanil. Do you know what that is?"

Matt nodded and said, "Yeah, I've heard of it but can't say I really know much about it."

Dr. Bridges continued, "I'm not surprised, we haven't seen carfentanil here in Franklin before. It took us a while to figure out what was in your system. It's a very powerful opioid. Think fentanyl, but much stronger. Veterinarians actually use it as an elephant tranquillizer. In its pure form, even trace amounts – about the size of a grain or two of sugar – can kill you."

"How in the world was I exposed to something like that?" Matt asked. "Everything was routine. The last thing I remember was leaving Duke's and getting in my car. I can recall driving away from Duke's - yeah, I was responding to a call downtown – but then it gets hazy after that."

"There's no telling how it happened. You could have inhaled it or touched it, and that's all it would take to get enough in your system to cause an OD or even death. You're damn lucky, Matt. If Lieutenant Tucker hadn't gotten a couple of doses of Narcan into you right away and that paramedic hadn't hung tough with the CPR, you'd be dead. They had to put two more doses of Narcan in you in the ambulance, and even that almost didn't work."

"What the hell did I hit when I blacked out? My chest hurts, it feels like I cracked some ribs."

Dr. Bridges laughed, "Nothing so dramatic, Matt. You weren't going very fast when you crashed. I heard that you plowed through some bushes that slowed the car down before you hit a tree. By then, you weren't moving fast enough to pop the airbag. The bruises are from the chest compressions when the paramedic performed CPR. She really had to work you over to keep you alive. If I were you, I'd do something nice for that paramedic. She did one hell of a job."

"You can count on that. I know that she likes wine, so I'll get her a really nice bottle."

From behind Dr. Bridges, a quiet, nervous feminine voice asked, "Doctor, is he going to be OK?"

Dr. Bridges hadn't noticed Erin, who had been at the back of the room retrieving something from her purse when she entered, and she turned to see who was speaking. Matt said, "Doctor, this is my fiancée, Erin. We were just engaged a couple of days ago. "

Dr. Bridges smiled and shook Erin's hand. "That's great news, congratulations. Well, I have some good news for both of you, then. Matt, all of your labs look good, and I think we can discharge you this afternoon if you'll have someone to keep an eye on you around the clock for a couple of days?"

Matt looked at Erin, who said "I can do that doctor, but I don't have any medical training – is that a problem?"

Dr. Bridges said, "No, just a precaution. I don't expect any problems at all, but it never hurts to be careful. And Matt, I want you to take a couple days off and just rest. Your body has been through a lot. No work, got it?"

Matt said, "Can I get that in writing? How about a week?"

Erin's voice suddenly became serious and she asked, "Wait a minute. How did this happen? Matt's not a drug user, and he doesn't remember anything happening that would have exposed him to, what did you call it?"

"That's a good question, and one that I've been wondering about. The drug is called carfentanil, and it's becoming a problem for first responders, like cops and paramedics. This stuff is so strong that you can OD just by skin contact, and sometimes Narcan doesn't work. Matt, is it possible that you were exposed during your shift?"

Matt thought for a second and then a sudden look of

recognition crossed his face. "I think I screwed up. When I came out of Duke's, there was something – it looked like a white powder - on the console in my car. I didn't give it any thought, I just brushed it off and started my rounds."

Dr. Bridges asked, "Think carefully Matt. Was the powder in your car before you went into the restaurant?"

"No, I'm sure it wasn't. I'm a bit of a neat freak, so I would have noticed something like that. But I don't have any idea how it got there."

"I'm guessing that you didn't lock your cruiser when you went into a Duke's?"

"No," Matt replied, "We don't usually have a problem with folks stealing cop cars."

"Well, I'm no detective, but it sure looks to me like someone planted it there while you were in Duke's."

Erin gasped, "My God, Matt, is someone trying to kill you?"

"I just don't know, Erin."

EIGHT

Cranberry Mall
11:30 A.M.

Cranberry Mall was a tired old structure, barely clinging to life, and that suited Cody's purpose well. The mall, a few miles north of Franklin, had opened in 1981 with great fanfare, and in its early years was a crowded, vibrant facility. But then, the companies that sustained the local economy shuttered their local manufacturing plants and moved away. The exodus of jobs doomed the local economy, and gradually the Cranberry Mall stores withered and died. The recent closing of the Sears store pretty much sealed the mall's fate, and today Cody was one of the few patrons in what seemed more like a dark, musty-smelling mausoleum than a place of business.

Cody was sitting at a corner table in an otherwise empty pizza shop, and things were not going according to plan. The only other person in the shop was a bored, middle-aged woman sitting behind the counter reading *Star* magazine in order to keep up with the latest celebrity gossip. The man that he was supposed to meet was 30 minutes late and not answering his phone. Cody nervously picked at a slice of plain cheese pizza and obsessively checked for text messages. *What the fuck is going on? Josh is always on time.*

The sound of a radio crackling interrupted Cody's thoughts, and when he looked up he saw two uniformed police officers approaching the shop. *What the hell? We had a deal, and I'm living up to my end of the bargain!* Cody tensed as the officers walked into the shop and looked directly at him before walking up to the counter and ordering a large pepperoni and two sodas. The officers paid and took their drinks to a table to await their pizza. *Oh, great. The only other people in the mall are two cops, and they decide to sit near me.* Unnerved, Cody reached for his soda but spilled it onto the table. Three tables away, the officers heard Cody quietly mutter "shit," and briefly looked at him before resuming their conversation.

As Cody used a thin paper napkin to dab at a spot of soda that had splashed on his shirt, he sensed someone else entering the shop and looked up to see Josh heading toward his table. Josh noticed the cops and, almost imperceptibly, slowed and shot a questioning look at Cody.

"Over here, Josh." Cody waved and Josh, having no choice, joined him. Cody was simultaneously relieved that his friend had arrived and nervous over the fact that the next several minutes could well determine whether he went to jail or walked. A bit too loudly, Cody said, "Let me finish my pizza and we can head out."

Several minutes later, Cody and Josh left the pizza shop and headed towards a secluded area near the closed Sears store. "Thanks for coming, Josh. I need to ask you a favor." Cody lowered his voice. "I need you to bring me to Pittsburgh, man. I gotta do some business."

Josh ignored the request and asked, "Cody, how the hell did you get out of jail? I thought they had your ass for sure."

"Pretty funny, actually. The cops knew what I was doing, but they didn't have any evidence. I didn't have anything on me - no drugs, no needles, nothing. The dealer never sold us anything; he just came up to the car and opened fire. You wouldn't believe how bad the cops tore my car apart trying to find some evidence. Then, they laid some bullshit on me about being charged with child endangerment. Even my dumbass lawyer wanted me to cop a plea, but I told them the only reason I was in the parking lot was to do a U-turn, and I didn't know anything about a drug buy. I threatened to sue their ass for false arrest and violating my civil rights – that's what they do on the TV shows. So here I am with the apologies of the Franklin PD – man, that pissed them off having to apologize for arresting me for something they knew I was doing but couldn't prove." Cody hoped that Josh didn't know about the prior warrant.

Josh slapped Cody's back and laughed, "You always did have a good line of BS, but I can't believe you pulled that one off. Way to go, dude. You doin' OK with Brandi getting blown away?"

That question hit Cody hard, and a weary look came across his face as he sighed, "Yeah, I guess. We hadn't been together very long, so I didn't really know her that well. The kid was pretty cute though, and I'm glad she's OK. I guess I was lucky, if you want to call it that, because when Brandi was killed I don't remember anything other than a muzzle flash and waking up in the ambulance. But can we get back to the favor I need?"

"OK, what kinda business are you talking about?"

"I need to buy a couple of bricks. I know you've got connections in Pittsburgh, Josh, you brought me there once before. It scared the crap outta me, though, when we made that buy."

Josh immediately understood what Cody had in mind. Because heroin was more expensive in rural areas like Franklin than in large cities, Cody could support his habit and earn some spending money by buying low in Pittsburgh and selling high in Franklin. He could buy a "brick" of 50 stamp bags (each containing more or less a single dose) for $300 in Pittsburgh and, after deducting Josh's 10-bag finder's fee for connecting him with a dealer and keeping twenty bags for his own use, could sell the remaining twenty bags for $400. That would cover the cost of a brick and leave him with $100 of spending money. He could also buy in bulk – they called it buying "weight" – at $120 per gram, but then he would need to cut and repackage each gram into 30 bags that he could sell.

"OK, but I can see a couple of problems with that Cody. First, you've got the cash? Those two bricks will set you back about $600, and I'm guessing that you don't have that kind of cash. And don't forget my finders' fee, I'm not about to risk my ass bringing you down there just for grins. "

"I've got about half the money. I was hoping to get someone to front me the rest."

"Good luck with that. No one's going to front you, and if you show up in Pittsburgh with your usual line of bullshit it won't end well. Those dudes are real serious. Do I need to remind you about the time that you tried to make a buy on your own and someone stuck a gun in your face and took your money?" Cody didn't think that Josh knew about that, and his face showed his surprise.

"I hear things, OK? Your second problem is that if you start selling here in Franklin, you're going to piss off some folks that you *really* don't want to piss off, you hear what I'm saying? They view Franklin as their turf, and if they hear you're dealing here they'll take you out in a heartbeat."

"I'm pretty desperate, man. I thought I could count on you."

Josh looked down and didn't respond for a minute. After obviously making up his mind, he looked back up at Cody, "I didn't say I won't help you. I'm just not going to get involved in something that might get us both killed. Look, I've got an idea. There's some people here in Franklin you could talk to, maybe work something out that's a win-win for both of you."

Cody said, "I'm listening."

Josh pulled his phone out of his pocket and said, "OK, let me make a few calls, and plan on meeting me right here tomorrow afternoon. I'll text you with the time. I'm going to introduce you to someone, but listen to me real good: don't bring an attitude with you."

"Damn it, I'm not sure that I can get out here. My car is still in the impound lot, and I don't have the cash to get it out, much less pay to fix the damage."

Josh gave Cody an impatient look before responding. "I'm not your goddamned mother, for Christ sakes. You're the one asking for a favor, so just figure it out, OK?" Josh turned and walked back into the mall, leaving Cody standing by himself.

NINE

C hief Miller was sitting in front of his television, but his attention was elsewhere. Miller's sole focus was on determining how he had been framed for a double murder, and what he could do to exonerate himself. Since handing over his badge last week he had slept only fitfully, and had neither left his house nor taken any phone calls. Dennis Archer had promised to slow play it as long as possible, and surprisingly the press hadn't called for his scalp. He knew that could change in a heartbeat.

As he sipped his coffee, his attention was drawn to the now familiar face of TV5 reporter Mercedes Boone standing in Fountain Park. A picture of Matt Riley was inset at the top corner of the screen. Miller grabbed the remote and turned up the volume.

"… Officer Riley will be released from the hospital this afternoon and is expected to recover fully. Our exclusive source tells us that someone planted an as-yet-unidentified drug in his patrol car, which caused Riley to black out and crash. The Franklin

Police Department has not responded to our request for a statement, and the UPMC Medical Center has declined to release any information on his condition. We're continuing our investigation and will provide further details as they become available."

Miller muted the TV and disgustedly flipped the remote on the couch. As he reached for his cell phone, he muttered to himself, "I may be on administrative leave, but someone should have shown me the courtesy of giving me a heads up on this." He quickly realized that the reason no one had called was that he had turned off his phone. When he turned it on, there were over twenty voice mails and texts, including several from Lieutenant Tucker. *I guess I turned it off so that I could focus on what I was doing. Oh, bullshit, you know better than that. You were feeling sorry for yourself and tried to shut out the world.*

He dialed Tucker's cell phone number from memory, and impatiently listened to four rings until it was answered. "Chief, where the hell have you been? I've been calling and texting you, and was just about to send a car to check on you. We've got a problem that I need to talk to you about."

Sheepishly, Miller said, "Sorry, I must have turned the phone off by accident. I just noticed it, and when I turned it on I saw your messages. Were you calling about Matt?"

"Yeah, I was hoping to talk to you before you heard about that. I just left the hospital, and he's going to be OK. But it was a close one. The doc said someone put some carfentanil in his cruiser, and he OD'd – we almost lost him. I was the first on the scene, when I pulled him out of the car I was exposed and it got to me too."

There was steel in Miller's voice when he said, "Are you telling me that this was intentional? Someone was trying to kill Matt?"

"Chief, it looks that way. If you don't mind a visitor, I'd like to stop by in about fifteen minutes and talk this through with you."

"Have you had lunch?"

Tucker said, "No. I can do that after we talk."

"Why don't you grab a couple of burgers on the way and we can talk here over lunch?

"Done. See you in fifteen."

TEN

Benjamin's Roadhouse
Thursday, December 28
12:30 P.M.

Sometimes things just work out by chance. Cody hadn't been thinking about lunch – he was far too depressed to be hungry – but as he was walking down Liberty Street he was drawn to Benjamin's Roadhouse because of its festive holiday decorations. Cody had always loved Christmas, and this year he was badly in need of a reminder of happier times. Just a month earlier – it felt like a lifetime ago – he had stood here on Liberty Street and watched the annual 'Light Up Night' celebration unfold. He remembered the parade led by Santa in a fire truck, the fireworks and, most of all, the joyous crowd. And then everything changed that night on Grant Street when he and Brandi had been shot.

He walked into Benjamin's, and the hostess sat him at a booth overlooking the courthouse. He was struck by the irony, given that the next chapter in his life would unfold inside that building. If he lived that long. Cody had never really paid much attention to the courthouse, but today it held a weird fascination for him. He studied the details of the three-story red brick building, and noticed for the first time the oddly unbalanced clock tower on one corner offset by a smaller cupola with a steep white dome on the opposite corner. He had heard somewhere that the building was erected in 1868 and was now listed on the National Register of Historic Places, but really didn't give a damn. All that mattered to him was what would happen there when they finally got around to bringing him to trial.

The waitress disrupted his thoughts when she walked up to the table and greeted him by name. Cody ignored the menu and placed his usual order of a steak and spinach salad, dressing on the side. Given the blustery weather, he opted for hot coffee rather than his usual diet soda. His meal arrived five minutes later, and he had barely started to eat when he heard the sound of an incoming text. He responded almost mechanically to the sound by pulling his iPhone out of his pocket.

"Meet me at mall main entrance at 1 PM," Josh.

Oh shit. I am screwed. There is no way that I can get to the mall by one. As he was considering that problem, a second text arrived,

"Come alone. Don't be late or meeting is off." Josh.

Cody's initial reaction was to laugh. *Yeah, right, like I might be able to get there in a half-hour.* Then he felt a rising sense of panic. The mall was seven miles away, he had no wheels or anyone that he could ask for a ride, and there was no cab service in Franklin. *If I blow this meeting, there goes my best shot at getting my ass out of a really big crack.*

Desperate, he bolted out of Benjamin's, leaving a

ten-dollar bill along with a half-full cup of coffee and most of his salad, and started jogging down Liberty Street. *What am I doing, in my condition I can't even run a mile.* In fact, he had barely covered two blocks when his legs weakened and his lungs started to burn. He stopped and bent over to catch his breath when a car pulled up beside him and a woman called his name. He turned to see who it was, and muttered to himself, "Un-fucking- believable. About time I caught a break."

Cody hopped into the car and greeted the driver with considerable enthusiasm, given that she could solve his immediate transportation problem. The two had dated off and on – mostly off – for the past several years, and it had been two months since he had seen her. Cody was physically attracted to her, but put off by the fact that she had three children by two different fathers. "Janice, how are you, it's great to see you. "

Janice smiled and said, "I'm doing fine, Cody, but where the hell have you been? I kept hoping you'd call or that we'd run into each other. But it's like you dropped off the face of the earth. Anyway, I haven't had lunch yet – maybe we could grab a quick bite and catch up?"

"I'd love to, Janice, but I've got to meet some dudes at the mall at one for some serious business. Can I get a rain check?"

"Sure, that works for me," Janice replied. "But if you're trying to get to the mall by one, why are you jogging down Liberty?"

"That's a damned good question, Janice, and here's where I need to ask you for a favor. The Mustang isn't running right now so I don't have any wheels." *Well, the truth is that it's in the police impound lot with a couple of shot out windows and blood all over it, but that's too much information for you right now.* "I was going to meet the guys later, but they moved it up on me. So, any chance you could run me out there?"

Janice thought for a second before replying, "Well . . . oh, what the hell, I don't have anything better to do. Let's go."

Fifteen minutes later, after subtly maneuvering Cody into asking her out to dinner the following night, Janice dropped him near the mall entrance. Cody glanced nervously at his watch, but relaxed when he realized that he was on time. As he entered the mall, he saw Josh standing just inside with a taller, harsh-looking man. Although the man's face was partially hidden by a Pittsburgh Steelers hat, he looked vaguely familiar. *Well, now I have a seat at the table – actually, I guess I've just found the table and need to talk my way into a seat.* As he approached Josh and the other man, Cody wiped a bead of sweat from his forehead.

Josh spoke first, "Nick, this is Cody, the guy I mentioned. Cody, this is Nick Jensen, and he may have a little work for you if he thinks you're a fit."

Nick looked at Cody appraisingly. "You're looking to deal? Scrawny little fucker, you sure don't look the part."

Cody replied coolly, "Looks can be deceiving. I know the business. But now that we're talking bona fides, I thought I knew — at least by reputation — all of the players in town, and I don't recall hearing your name before."

Josh cringed at this challenge, knowing full well that Nick wouldn't tolerate it. The only question was how violent the reaction would be. That question was answered by a sudden blur as Nick punched Cody in the face with enough force to knock him off of his feet. "Wise ass, huh. I should just burn your ass, kid."

As Cody looked up from the ground, his eyes were watering and a trickle of blood ran from his lip and down his chin. Cody slowly pushed himself to his feet and, with far more confidence than he felt, laughed and said, "Who was the guy that said, after spitting out a couple of his teeth, 'I've had my ass kicked by better men than you?' So, are we gonna do some business or what?"

Nick starred at Cody incredulously, and then broke into a huge grin. "Well, you keep your cool, and that's a good thing. I think I'm going to call you Timex – you take a lickin and keep on tickin. So, to answer your question, you might say I'm the new sheriff in town. You may have noticed that some of the familiar faces aren't around anymore?"

"Yeah, I wondered what happened."

Nick nodded towards the door and said, "Let's take a walk." With Nick leading, the trio headed out into the parking lot and found Nick's car, a black Cadillac Escalade with heavily tinted windows. Nick motioned Cody into the front passenger seat and, looking at Josh, nodded to the rear passenger seat. Nick settled into the driver's seat and turned to Cody, "Josh tells me that you're looking to make a little money."

Cody glanced at Josh and then responded, "Yeah, and he told me that dealing in Franklin wasn't a good idea because I might offend some people that I didn't want to offend."

"He told you right. *I'm* the people that you don't want to offend."

Nick turned to Josh and asked pointedly, "Before I go any further, last chance, are you sure this guy's OK?"

"Yeah, I've known him a long time, and we can trust him.

Like I said, he's pretty quick on his feet. You heard about the guy that MF drilled?"

"Yeah, what ever happened to him? Last I heard he was in the hospital getting a hole in his head plugged."

"You're looking at him." Both Cody and Nick looked at Josh in surprise. Before either could respond, Josh continued, "What came down was that Cody played it cool. The cops pulled his car apart and didn't find anything – no drugs, no needles, they didn't find jack shit. They turned the screws on Cody, but he claimed he was just a poor innocent dude doing a U turn when someone shot him and the girl. He hung tough with that story. They didn't believe a fucking word of it, but they couldn't prove anything and he walked."

Nick looked at Josh and said, "you might have mentioned that to me, asshole, before you set this up. Well, at least we know he's not a cop. But, if he's dumb enough to bring a kid on a buy, for Christsakes…"

Cody, finally grasping the meaning of what Josh had just said, yelled, "Hey, wait just a fucking minute! Who the hell is MF and what do you mean he drilled me?"

Nick and Josh were both momentarily confused by Cody's anger, and when they realized that he had no clue who had shot him or why they both broke into hysterical laughter.

"Oh, shit. I guess you wouldn't know, would you," Nick said. "MF was an enforcer - his real name was Myron Foley – and he was filling in for a dealer that night. Anyway, your bad luck, you showed up in that parking lot at exactly the wrong time with MF's ex-girlfriend. Except, he didn't consider her to be an 'ex' and the kid you had with you was his. MF wasn't what you'd call real understanding about those sorts of things. Getting the picture?"

"You've got to be kidding me! I never knew what the hell happened. I thought it was probably someone trying to rip me off. Hey, you said his name 'was' Myron?"

Nick said, "Yeah, someone used him for target practice with a shotgun and then tossed him in the river."

"Is that one of the guys the police chief killed?"

"Don't believe everything that you hear. 'Ol Chief Miller – man, someone set his ass up good. What I heard was the guys running things in Pittsburgh were pretty pissed about the whole thing, and decided to deal with MF and have a little fun while they were at it." Nick shook his head and laughed, "You have to admit, offing those two and making it look like a cop did it was pure fucking artistry. Now enough of the questions, you already know more than you need to."

Nick paused for a minute while he thought about what he wanted to do. "Timex, I tell you what I need. I've got people who can move my merchandise, and you wouldn't be very good at it anyway. But what I don't have is someone to help Josh keep things organized, if you know what I mean. We're doing a lot of business, and things are getting a little out of control. Josh says you're good at that sorta thing. True?"

"Yeah, I can do that," Cody replied. "I used to work in a restaurant – scheduling people, ordering supplies, that sort of thing – same shit, different business."

"Yeah, whatever, I guess you'll do. So, here's the deal. I'm gonna make you Josh's gopher. You do what he tells you, when he tells you do it. He tells you to sweep the floors, you sweep the fucking floors. He tells you to count the cash, you count the fucking cash. Got it?" Cody nodded. "But one thing you gotta know right up front. You cross me in any way; you turn up short on inventory; some cash turns up missing; you bring us any unwanted attention — I'll cut your balls off with a rusty knife and feed them to you. Understood?"

"Yeah, understood."

"OK, we'll try it. Since you already know too much, you don't want to know what happens if you don't work out."

That decision made, Nick visibly relaxed and said, "Josh, why don't you give him a ride home?" He turned to Cody and said, "We were wondering how you'd get here in a half hour with no wheels." Nick pulled out a wad of bills, peeled one off and handed it to Josh. "When Josh said you'd talk your way into a ride, I called bullshit and bet him you wouldn't. That just cost me $100. Anyway, Josh will fill you in on what we want you to do." Nick peeled off more bills from his wad and handed them to Cody, "And get your car fixed, for Chrissakes. You'd look pretty silly riding around town on a bicycle. That would be bad for our image." Nick laughed at his own wit, and then motioned for Cody and Josh to get out of the car.

As they walked away from Nick's SUV, Josh said, "Cody, I just put my ass on the line for you. Don't fuck it up."

"Thanks, Josh. I owe you big time, and I won't let you down." *What the hell have I gotten myself into? Either I screw Josh and Nick, which could get me killed, or I go to jail for a real long time. Which could also get me killed. Then again, Josh hasn't been completely straight with me.* "By the way, you knew what happened the night I was shot?"

"Yeah, but I didn't think you needed to know that. I'm in this a little deeper than I let on to you. But I had to bring it up today because if I didn't tell Nick that you were the one that

MF shot, and he found out later, he'd be really pissed. As you might have noticed, Nick has a bit of a temper."

Cody made a show of rubbing his jaw and said, "No shit. That would have been good to know earlier. Josh, I think we better agree to level with each other from here on out." *Well, other than the fact that I'm a CI. I think that I'll keep that to myself.*

"Yeah, that might just keep both of us alive."

"And what's that crap about Pittsburgh people?"

"Come on, I know some of this is new to you, but you don't really think Nick is calling the shots, do you? Wake up, dude. We're just a flea on the tail of the dog. There's some people in Pittsburgh who run the show – only Nick knows who they are, and I'm not sure that he has the complete picture. The word I hear is that the Pittsburgh gang is controlled by the Mexicans. Now, enough of the questions, you're getting to the point where you're going from curious to flat ass dangerous."

Josh pointed out his car and said to Cody, "Get in, I'll give you a ride home."

ELEVEN

Fountain Park

4 P.M.

Cody was sitting on a park bench near where Matt had crashed and, as he looked at the tire tracks across the grass and the damaged bushes, the irony of what he had to do was not lost on him. He started to dial his cell phone for the fourth time in the last two hours, hesitated, and then put it back in his pocket. *Damn it, this is not good. I really don't want to make this call, but not calling isn't an option.* Finally he pulled the phone from his pocket and made the call.

After several rings, he heard a recorded voice say, "Hi, this is Matt Riley. You know the drill," followed by a tone.

"Matt, this is Cody. You know the number. We have to talk . . . it's important. Call me." Cody ended the call and started to walk towards Liberty Street. *That's just great. I don't even know if Matt is back on his feet again. Now what do I do? I don't trust any of the other cops, and the DA made it real clear that he doesn't want any part of me.*

As Cody considered his options his phone rang, startling him. He looked at the caller ID, and was relieved when he saw the number. "Matt, thanks for calling back. I was afraid that you were still laid up."

"Nah, the phone was just in another room and I couldn't get to it before it rolled over to voice mail. So, what's up?"

"I heard some things that you ought to know about. It's not much, but maybe it's a start."

"OK," Matt said evenly, "Tell me what you have."

"Well, I just met the guy who claims that he's now running heroin distribution in Franklin. I'm not sure if he was blowing smoke up my ass, but what he said was that people in Pittsburgh are calling the shots and they decided to clean house here. Anyway, he sounded like the real deal to me."

"Cody, I'm having a hard time believing that you just happened to run into someone like that. Besides, you're supposed to be doing what we tell you, not free-lancing. You'd better explain what happened."

"It's a long story, but the short version is that I asked an old friend to see about making some connections, and he set up a meet at the mall with a guy named Nick. I've never heard of him, but he seems like a serious dude."

"What do you mean serious?"

"I guess you had to be there to understand. Have you ever met someone that you just knew was dangerous the minute you laid eyes on them? The sort of guy you just don't want to mess with?"

Matt laughed, "Oh, yeah. When I was in the Marines there were a few guys that I could tell just from looking at them were walking death."

"Exactly. Well, Nick is one of those guys. He kinda confirmed my suspicions when he didn't like something I said and knocked me flat on my ass. It got a bit scary for a minute, but after a while we chilled out. Anyway, it turns out that my friend is real close to this guy, maybe his number two, and he needs someone to help. The way Nick put it, I'll be a 'gopher.' So, if this is for real, I'll be on the inside and might hear some interesting things. But, I should add that Nick gave me a very inspirational speech on what would happen to me if I crossed him."

Matt replied, "Cody, you knew going into this that it would be dangerous. For starters, you need to dial back the smart-ass so that people will quit using you for a punching bag. And even with that, you're going to have to be damned careful not to blow your cover. We'll talk about that later, but did you learn anything else?"

Cody said, "Hell yeah. On a real personal level, I now know what happened the night that I got shot. Have you figured anything out on that yet?"

"Nothing solid, we're still following leads on that."

"Leads my ass, you've got nothing. What happened is that I got sideways with a guy named "MF." His real name is Myron Foley – can you believe that, Myron fucking Foley. Seems that I showed up in that parking lot with his girlfriend and his daughter – Daisy was his. He blew his cool and shot us."

Matt said, "I know who you're talking about, and he's bad news. I think it's time that I had a little chat with him."

Cody laughed, "Yeah, well don't waste your time on that. Apparently, you haven't ID'd the two people that you fished out of the river, right"

"No," Matt said defensively, "but we're working on it, and should have something pretty soon."

"One of them was MF. I don't know who the other one was."

"Are you sure about that?"

"I'm just telling you what I heard, man. You're the cop, you go figure it out. But I got something else that's a bit personal for *you*. The word is that the two dead guys that were handcuffed together weren't murdered by your police chief. Nick heard that someone from Pittsburgh set him up. The people that did it are laughing their asses off over this."

Matt was stunned. After a minute, he said, "How the hell did they pull that off? I need to know everything that you heard, even things that you think don't matter."

"I really don't know. I just listened to what they were saying. Asking questions would have been really dumb, so I let it go."

"Yeah, I see your point. Look, I'm tied up right now, but let's meet tomorrow. I'll text you with a time and place."

Cody said, "OK, but let's not make it too public. If the wrong people see me with you, I'm a dead man." With that, Cody hung up and walked out of the park.

SECTION VI
A TEST OF WILLS

ONE

Mayor Kelliher, sitting at the head of a large conference table, nodded as Dennis Archer entered the room a few minutes before their 8 AM meeting. Kelliher put down the cup of coffee that he was drinking and arrogantly ordered, "Grab a seat Archer. As soon as Lieutenant Tucker finds time in his busy schedule to join us we can get started. This won't take very long, I just want to be sure that we're all on the same page about the nonsense I'm hearing about a so-called drug problem in Franklin."

At precisely 8 AM, Lieutenant Tucker and an unexpected guest walked into the conference room and sat at the opposite end of the table from Kelliher. The guest glared at Kelliher and said defiantly, "I'll be joining Lieutenant Tucker this morning." Kelliher exploded, "What the *hell* are *you* doing here, Miller? You weren't invited to this meeting, and you're supposed to be on administrative leave pending Archer filing murder charges against you. This is an outrage!"

Dennis Archer responded to Kelliher's challenge. "I'll answer that, Walter. There've been some new developments that

I need to fill you in on. As you know, Chief Miller initially was the prime suspect in the double homicide. We've been conducting an around-the-clock investigation since the bodies were found, and here's what we've come up with. First, the coroner has determined that the time of death was between 9 PM and midnight on Wednesday, December 20. She based that conclusion on her own examination as well as testimony by witnesses who saw both victims alive that night at 9 PM. Second, we know that Chief Miller was nowhere near the scene of the murder at any time from noon until well after midnight. Several reliable witnesses have established his whereabouts during that period. So, while I *don't* know how the murderer got the Chief's pistol and handcuffs, I *do* know that the Chief is not the killer. Given that, this morning I told the Chief that he is no longer a suspect and there is no reason for him not to resume his duties."

"You can't do that," Kelliher screamed. "I had your word that charges would be filed! A deal is a deal, Archer. I don't give a rat's ass about your so-called new evidence."

Archer was amused by Kelliher's outburst, and calmly responded, "This isn't one of your sleazy political deals, Walter, it's about justice. I'm not in the business of trying to get convictions just to add another notch to my belt or to further your political agenda. My job is to be sure that when my office seeks a conviction we have evidence that the individual is really guilty. I just explained to you that we have new evidence that exonerates Chief Miller, and therefore I have no intention of filing any charges against him." Kelliher's face turned bright red, but before he could speak, Archer turned to Miller and said, "Chief, do you have anything to add?"

"Yes, thanks Dennis. Now that we've cleared the air on that, it's past time that we focused on the opioid problem here in Franklin. Over the last week or so this has become a full-blown crisis. So, to start with, I've asked Dr. Bridges to join us to give us a medical perspective. I've also asked Matt Riley to join us because I've appointed him to lead our efforts to deal with this crisis." Miller turned toward the door and called out, "Matt, Dr. Bridges, we're ready for you now."

Kelliher slammed his hand on the table and shouted, "You're not appointing anyone to anything, Miller. The only crisis we have is a police chief that thinks he's above the law. As far as I'm concerned, you're still on administrative leave and have no authority whatsoever. So, either get out of my conference room right now or you're fired."

Archer looked at Kelliher and said in an exasperated tone, "Walter, I figured you might try something like this, so I've looked into it and you do *not* have the authority to fire Chief Miller. That would have to be done by the City Manager with the approval of the City Council. I've spoken to the City Manager and each of the Council members, and no one will support firing the Chief. So, Walter, kindly cut the bullshit and let the Chief continue."

"Who the hell do you think you are, Archer. You can't speak to me that way, I'm the Mayor of this city."

"Walter, unless you sit there quietly while we try to make sense of what's going on, we'll move this meeting to my office and proceed without you. Let me be perfectly clear on this. If we have to take that step, I'll make sure that the press learns that the Chief and I don't trust you and have excluded you from our discussions. You should also understand that, if I have to take that step, the City Council is prepared to vote unanimously to remove you from office. Now, I'll admit, the law is at best unclear on whether they can do that, but I don't think you want to go down that road. So, your call Walter – and a simple yes or no is all that I want to hear from you – do you want to do it my way or not?"

A flood of emotions crossed Kelliher's face as he considered his options and finally realized that he had been backed into a corner. As that realization dawned on him, he looked down at the table dejectedly and mumbled, "Yeah, get on with it."

Archer turned to Miller and said calmly, "Chief, please continue."

"Thank you, Dennis. My thinking is this. The first thing we should do is have Dr. Bridges brief us about the drug that's caused our recent wave of fatalities. Next, I want to hear from Matt on whether he's turned up anything on how the drug is being brought into Franklin, and get his thoughts on how we can shut that pipeline down as soon as possible. Finally, Dennis, I need to hear from you concerning our legal options. Can anybody think of anything else that we need to cover?"

Miller looked around the table and saw that no one else had anything to add. "OK, Dr. Bridges, thank you for joining us this morning. The floor is yours."

Dr. Bridges stood at the end of the table furthest from Kelliher and began, "I think the place to start is with an overview of what we're facing. You probably know most of this, but let's cover the basics just to be sure. We're dealing with a serious opioid problem nationally – in 2018 nearly 70,000 Americans died from drug overdoses, and seventy percent of those were from opioids. That's more drug deaths in a year than the number of Americans who died during the entire ten years of the Vietnam War! What's happening here in Franklin is a reflection of that problem."

Heads nodded around the table, indicating that everyone was aware of the scope of the opioid problem.

"So, let's start with what are opioids and how do they work. Opioids include a number of legitimate prescription drugs, such as Oxycodone, Percocet and Vicodin, as well as various illicit drugs that are found on the street, such as heroin and fentanyl. Most people don't know that heroin was actually developed by one of the big pharma companies, Bayer, as a 'less-addictive' alternative to morphine." The reference to heroin as "less addictive" drew hoots of derisive laughter from the group.

Dr. Bridges continued, "It's really not that funny, guys. Much of the current opioid crisis has its roots in legitimate prescription pain relievers, but I'll get to that in a minute. The way opioids work is that they bind to what are called opioid receptors in the brain in a way that inhibits pain and typically induces euphoria. The problem is that opioids are highly addictive. Once someone gets hooked, they will do just about anything to get their next fix."

Matt raised his hand, as if he was in a class, and Dr. Bridges smiled and said, "Matt, you have a question?"

"Yes, I'm a little confused. If doctors have been prescribing these pain relievers, doesn't that mean that they're safe? I mean, surely doctors wouldn't have prescribed something that would hurt people?"

"I hate to say this, Matt, but that's simply not true. Through the 1980s, doctors used opioids mostly for cancer pain relief, and were very careful about prescribing them for anything else because of the fear of addiction. But the problems began in the 90s, when the medical profession started talking about pain as being the 'fifth vital sign.' Doctors began to focus more on eliminating pain and downplayed the risks of addiction. At the same time, the pharmaceutical companies started aggressively pushing opioids for post-surgical pain, back pain, arthritis and seemingly every other pain you can imagine."

Dr. Bridges paused for a second to gather her thoughts. "The use of prescription opioids really spiraled out of control when OxyContin came along, and one of the big pharma companies claimed that because it was a time-release drug the chance of addiction was minimal. That was a lie, and they damn well knew it. OxyContin became one of the most prescribed narcotics in the country, and Purdue alone has made over $35 billion in sales from OxyContin since it began marketing the drug in 1996."

She continued, "Needless to say, the pharma companies put major marketing efforts into OxyContin – they paid huge bonuses to their sales reps to push the stuff, and they aggressively pushed doctors to prescribe it by using tactics like offering all-expense paid trips to "seminars" at resorts to high prescribers. Unfortunately, many doctors fell for the marketing gimmicks, so if you went to the doctor – or the dentist – with pain, real or imagined, they handed opioids out like candy. Just to give you an idea, opioid prescriptions increased tenfold from 1990 to 2015. Almost a quarter of people on opioids for non-cancer pain became hooked on them, and half the OD deaths were caused by prescription opioids. The irony is that opioids aren't even that effective at mitigating many of the types of pain for which they're being prescribed."

Matt asked, "Then why hasn't anyone done anything about it?"

Dr. Bridges continued, "When everyone is making enough money I guess people hide their heads in the sand. But, the tide is starting to turn. In 2007, Purdue paid about $600 million to settle a lawsuit that asserted that they misled everyone concerning the risk of addiction, and three of their executives pled guilty to criminal charges. That was too little and too late, and it sure didn't stem the tidal wave of addictions."

Archer interjected, "And recently state and local governments have filed lawsuits against the opioid manufacturers seeking around $80 billion in damages. The strategy that they're using is pretty much what they used against the tobacco manufacturers, although this will be a little more complicated since the federal regulators approved the prescription opioid drugs as safe."

Chief Miller grunted and asked, "But how in the hell are we going to stop this if we're dealing with legal prescriptions?"

Dr. Bridges responded, "Chief, the biggest problem that you're facing is illegal opioids on the street. We've already made good progress on dialing back on opioid prescriptions and shutting down the pill mills. But, cutting back on legal opioids has created a different, and in some ways more difficult, set of problems. As prescription painkillers have become harder to get – and more expensive – people who were addicted didn't just stop using them. No, they turned to street heroin. If you know where to look, anyone – even school kids – can get heroin. At least with the prescription drugs people knew what they were getting, but with street heroin there's no telling what they're getting in terms of strength and purity."

Chief Miller said, "That makes sense. But, we've been dealing with heroin on the streets for several years, so why are we suddenly seeing a wave of fatal ODs?"

"Chief, the problem is we now have a more potent type of drug than you usually find on the street. If you think about it, your typical addict has a pretty good idea of the dose that they need to get their high. Even so, they still can overdose. What we're seeing now is a powerful new substance called 'Ace of Diamonds,' which is heroin cut with a high proportion of a powerful synthetic opioid called fentanyl. That's a game changer. If an addict doesn't know what they're getting and takes a normal dose of this stuff… well, you've seen the results."

Dr. Bridges paused to gather her thoughts and then asked, "You're all generally familiar with fentanyl, right?" When everyone nodded yes, she continued. "Fentanyl is about fifty times stronger than heroin – to give you an idea of how potent it is, as little as 2 – 3 milligrams of pure fentanyl can cause respiratory depression and possibly death. Now, bear in mind that there are legitimate uses for prescription fentanyl, such as for the relief of cancer-related pain, but what we're seeing on the street is typically cheap synthetic fentanyl imported illegally from China."

Dennis Archer interjected, "I understand that it was an even more powerful drug that almost killed Matt. How does that come into play?"

"That's correct, Dennis. What we found in Matt's body, and what was later discovered in trace amounts in his car, was something called carfentanil. That drug was developed to tranquilize elephants. Think about how powerful that has to be. Exposure to trace amounts of this drug can be enough to kill a human. In Matt's case, it looks like they mixed it with some talcum powder and sprinkled it in his car. I can tell you this – that was no accident, someone was trying to kill Matt."

Matt asked, "How do first responders know when we're facing something like this, and how do we protect ourselves?"

"That's a tough one, Matt. You're going to have to be super cautious. You've already been taught to wear gloves, eye protection and masks when there's any doubt. But that's no longer enough. The reality is that if there is *any* indication that there are drugs involved in a crime scene or a traffic stop, you'll need to back off and treat it like a hazmat scene. That means someone with training and full personal protective equipment will have to respond. I'm not trying to be critical, but the way that Matt's situation was handled shows that it's time for refresher training."

Miller asked, "So, doctor, from your medical perspective, how do we keep this Ace of Diamonds from killing more people?"

"Chief, I've been doing a lot of research on what's helped with the opioid problem in other cities, and I think it comes down to a three-prong approach. First, we need to reduce the supply. That's something that will have an immediate impact in saving lives, and that's your job and Mr. Archer's. But arresting and locking up the dealers and the users isn't going to solve the problem by itself. Second, we need to work on prevention and education in the community. In other words, we need to provide useful information to people about the danger of drug abuse, and provide resources for people who are abusing. Finally, we need to make treatment options available for addicts."

Miller said, "That's a lot to think about, and some of it's long term, so I think we better figure out our priorities. To start with, how about you and I get together this afternoon to work out the first responder training so that we can get that out to the field ASAP."

Dr. Bridges said, "Sure, that's a good starting point. I'm pretty flexible this afternoon, so just let me know when."

"OK. Next, let's talk about how to quickly shut down the Ace of Diamonds pipeline." Chief Miller turned to Matt and said, "You're up next. I realize that I've just asked you to take the lead on this. I don't expect that you've turned up anything so far, but I do want to hear about how you plan to approach the problem."

"Sure, Chief. Well, first off, I do have some developments to report. We've actually had a pretty good break – we have a confidential informant who has already given us some good information. We've assigned him the code name of Agent Blue. To start with, he was able to identify one of the two victims that you were initially suspected of killing, and explain why they were killed."

"Whoa, now you have my full attention. I want to hear everything that you heard on that subject."

Kelliher interrupted, "Just a minute, Miller. Officer Riley, you *will* begin your answer by identifying your so-called Agent Blue. I want a name."

Dennis Archer, having finally exhausted his patience, snapped at the Mayor. "Walter, we agreed on the rules for this meeting and you just violated them. So, the first thing I have to say is that you will not under any circumstances be made privy to the identity of Agent Blue. For what should be obvious reasons that information is very sensitive, and it will be restricted to me, Lieutenant Tucker, Matt and – now that he is back on duty – Chief Miller. The second thing that I have to say is that this meeting is adjourned. Except for the Mayor, who will not be joining us, and who will no longer have access to what this group is doing, we will reconvene in my office in fifteen minutes. Chief, will you please station an officer outside of my office and instruct him to arrest Mayor Kelliher if he tries to enter?"

"Yes, sir. Consider it done."

Archer stared at Kelliher for a full thirty seconds, defying him to protest his exclusion from the meeting. The others shifted uncomfortably in their chairs as they waited to see how this confrontation would end. At first Kelliher glared angrily at Archer, but then he suddenly jumped from his chair and rushed towards him while screaming, "That does it, I'm going to kick your sorry ass right here and right now."

Matt was sitting between the two, and he quickly stood up and grabbed Kelliher firmly by the shoulders to restrain him. Kelliher struggled to escape Matt's grasp, and when that failed he attempted to knee Matt in the crotch. Matt easily deflected Kelliher's knee, and then with his left hand grasped Kelliher's right thumb in a way that bent it back unnaturally and brought the mayor to his knees yelping in pain. Matt calmly said, "Mr. Mayor, please control yourself or I'll have to place you under arrest."

While the others in the room were trying to stifle smiles, Kelliher looked up at Matt and pleaded, "OK, OK, please, let me go. You're hurting me."

Matt tightened his hold slightly to emphasize the point he

was about to make, eliciting a gasp of pain from the Mayor, and said calmly, "I'm going to let you go, and you *will* go back to your seat and stay there until we're gone. If you don't, I'm going to ask everyone else to leave the room so that you and I can continue this discussion. Understood?"

Kelliher, now with a frightened look on his face, screamed, "Yes, yes, let me go."

Matt maintained his hold for another few seconds while looking Kelliher directly in the eye, and then finally released him. Matt watched him walk back to his seat, gingerly massaging his thumb. He then turned to the others and said, "I believe the Mayor has nothing further to say, so maybe we should head over to Mr. Archer's office."

Archer could no longer contain his laughter at Kelliher sitting red-faced in his chair looking like a whipped puppy, and that started a chain reaction among the others. "Yes, Walter does seem to be unnaturally quiet. Let's all grab some coffee and reconvene in fifteen."

◆

Mayor Walter Kelliher was beyond pissed off. He was still sitting at the conference table in his office, fuming over the fact that Dennis Archer had moved the meeting and threatened to arrest him if he dared try to rejoin it. And that goddamned Chief Miller had gone along with Archer and agreed to station one of his cops outside the DA's office. And to top it off, that dim-witted, knuckle-dragging ex-Marine asshole had just about ripped his thumb off. *I'll have their asses, all of them.*

The bastards had even refused to tell him the name of their Confidential Informant. What a bunch of bullshit, acting like it was such a secret that they couldn't tell the fucking Mayor of the fucking town of Franklin the name of the fucking CI. Well, their plans were going to blow up in their arrogant faces. Let them have their private meeting, he would handle matters his own way. Kelliher slammed his mug on the table so hard that it shattered, opening a small cut on his hand and showering coffee onto the table and his shirt.

As he angrily blotted the coffee from his shirt an idea began to form in his mind. Without fully thinking it through, Kelliher reached for the phone and dialed a number from memory; he had been given strict instructions to never write this number down, and not to call unless it was important. Only after the phone started to ring did he begin to consider that there might be some downsides to what he was about to do. Kelliher was not the least bit concerned about the morality of his actions; his only concern was that he have his revenge. After the third ring a quiet voice with a heavy Eastern European accent answered, "Hello, Walter. I'm surprised to hear from you." Kelliher recoiled when he heard those words. He wondered whether his fearful reaction was to the cold, emotionless voice itself, or to the messenger of death who uttered the words.

"I have some information that I think you'll find useful," Kelliher said.

"What is it?"

"I just learned that the police have a confidential informant in your Franklin operation. This is something new, and I don't have a name yet."

There was a silent pause, long enough to make Kelliher wonder if the connection had been broken, when the voice continued, "It's time that you earned the money that we have paid you. Get me the name."

Kelliher, beginning to recognize the trap that he had walked into, responded in a whinny voice. "I, ah, don't know if I can do that. I demanded the name but they all refused to give it to me. They're calling him Agent Blue, but that's all I have. They acted like they don't trust me. That's why I called you. I thought if you knew what was going on you could figure out who this Agent Blue is on your end."

The voice responded with a harshness, almost a hiss, that terrified Kelliher, "Get that name for me by tomorrow or we will no longer require your services. Now, tell me everything that you know about this Agent Blue."

This conversation was not going the way that Kelliher had planned. His voice began to quiver as it dawned on him that instead of getting back at Archer he had instead placed himself in very real danger. "I know that one of our officers by the name of Matt Riley is running the CI. I think if you take care of Riley, you'll scare off the CI and take care of the problem. The CI gave Riley the name of one of the two people that were found in the river, and explained why they were killed but not who killed them. He also mentioned that someone in Pittsburgh ordered the killings. I'll do what I can to find out the name of the CI, but I can't promise anything."

The voice said, "Get me the name by tomorrow." And with that, the line went dead.

TWO

As the group left City Hall, Archer said "What the hell was that, Matt? I've never seen that move before."

"No big deal, just a technique they taught us in the Corps. It's amazing the amount of pain that you can cause just by bending a joint the wrong way. It works especially well on people like the Mayor, who have a low pain threshold. His thumb will be sore for a couple of days, but I don't think there will be any permanent damage."

Archer chuckled, "But his dignity will take longer to heal. Nicely done, I would have bought a ticket to watch him grovel like that. I've got a few more people I'd like to see you do that to." Seeing the serious look on Matt's face, Archer quickly added, "Just kidding, of course. Anyway, now that the entertainment part of the program is over, I've got my car here if anyone wants a ride over to the courthouse?"

Lieutenant Tucker accepted the invitation just as the sound of an incoming text caused Dr. Bridges to look at her phone. "I've got to get back to the hospital – one of my patients has had a setback. Chief, I'll call you when I break loose."

"OK, Doctor, I'll talk with you later." Chief Miller turned to Archer and said, "Dennis, Matt and I will walk to your office. I want to get a decent cup of coffee, not the industrial effluent that you drink."

Archer feigned offense and said, "You don't know good coffee. But, suit yourself. Go get your fancy gourmet coffee, and then you can join us uncultured slobs. Let's plan on starting at nine."

Matt and the Chief walked together in a comfortable silence for two blocks, each processing what had just happened and forming their thoughts. When they reached Fountain Park, where Matt had nearly died the previous week, Miller stopped walking and broke the silence. "I've been thinking about how to say this, but I may as well just be blunt. I don't trust Kelliher as far as I can throw him. My gut tells me that he's up to something dirty, but I don't have anything concrete to back that up."

"I have the same gut feeling, Chief. A part of me wanted to 'accidentally' break his wrist when I was restraining him, partly to teach him a lesson, but mostly for personal satisfaction. So, what do we do about him?"

"Honestly, right now there isn't a damn thing that we can do without some evidence that's he's dirty. And no, you can't break his arm, no matter how much I'd personally like to see that. I'm just saying, keep your guard up when you're around him."

"You can count on it, Chief."

Miller continued, "What we need to focus on is keeping your CI alive and getting as much useful information as we can from him. We have to cut this Ace of Diamonds problem off fast, and your guy could be the key. I was thinking that we may have enough from your CI to get a warrant on this Nick character – let's raise that with the DA. But first, let's grab some decent coffee at Epoch; we can continue this conversation in Archer's office."

Five minutes later, the Chief and Matt walked into Archer's office with coffee in hand and sat down. Archer looked at the two of them and said with mock sternness, "Well, now that you've fed your caffeine addiction, perhaps we can proceed?" Miller, smiling, gave Archer the finger.

Archer shook his head and said, "My, someone is in a bad mood this morning. And I so hoped that we could all be friends." After some affected laughter, Archer turned serious. "OK, let's get on with it. I had hoped that we could avoid that ridiculous scene with the Mayor, but he just can't seem to control himself. Before we get started, I want to mention that I'm a little concerned that Kelliher has been pumping me for information lately, asking for details of some ongoing investigations that he really doesn't need to know. I may just be paranoid, but I want to make sure that the details of what we discuss will not be shared with him. As a wise man once said, just because you're paranoid doesn't mean that there aren't little green men with machetes following you around." Archer looked at each of them in turn, "Are we all agreed? Not a single thing that we discuss gets repeated to Kelliher, no matter what he demands or threatens?"

Miller responded, "For sure, Dennis. Matt and I just had the same conversation on the way over here, and we both have a gut feeling that Kelliher is up to something. Nothing that we can put a finger on, mind you, but something just feels wrong there."

"Ok, good. It's not just me. By the way, Dr. Bridges does not need to know – doesn't want to know – the identity of our CI. I don't need to explain to you guys that if his identity gets out he'll be in serious danger. If anyone starts asking questions about the CI's identity, Chief Miller and I need to know about it immediately. Any questions on that point?" There were no questions, so Archer turned to Matt. "The floor is yours, Matt."

"Thank you. Chief, has anyone told you the name of our CI?"

Miller laughed. "No, Matt. I've only been out of the doghouse for a couple of hours. I suspect that there are a lot of things that I need to get caught up on."

"OK, the CI is Cody Ware, and yes, it's the same Cody Ware that was involved in the shooting at the Grant Street mall." Chief Miller nodded thoughtfully and motioned for Matt to continue.

"I'm a little worried that Cody is in over his head. I think he's basically a decent guy, but good judgment isn't his strong suit and he's a world-class smart-ass. But, I feel responsible for him since I dragged him into this, and I want to be sure that we don't leave his ass hanging out in the breeze."

"Anyway, as I started to say before we voted the Mayor off the island, Cody is in with a guy named Nick Jensen, who seems to be controlling heroin distribution here in Franklin. This guy hasn't been on our radar screen up to now, so we don't know anything about him. According to Cody, Nick thinks that someone in Pittsburgh ordered the murders. Apparently, the folks in Pittsburgh thought it was hilarious the way they set you up Chief, even though they knew it would come out pretty quickly that you had nothing to do with it."

Chief Miller snarled, "We'll see who has the last laugh. When I find out who the bastard was that broke into my house, stole my pistol and handcuffs and made a damned fool out of me, maybe we'll have another body floating in the river."

"Chief," Archer said warningly, "I know that you're only speaking figuratively, but you need to knock it off. You'd be amazed how that sort of thing can come back to bite you if the wrong person hears it, like that lady reporter. I can see the TV5 news headline now, 'Franklin Police Chief threatens to kill respected local pharmaceutical salesman.' Christ, that's all we need."

"OK, I hear you. Go on, Matt, what else have you learned?"

"Cody also told me that one of the 'victims' was a guy named Myron Foley – he went by 'MF' – but he didn't know about the other one. And, MF is the guy who shot Cody and his girlfriend Brandi Jennings last week. It turns out that MF was Jennings' ex-boyfriend and the little girl's father. He saw them in the car with another guy and went nuts."

Chief Miller said, "Well, that explains why the shooting happened. It just didn't make sense until you put that piece of the puzzle on the table. Did your CI say anything about Ace of Diamonds?"

"Yes, I was about to get to that. Cody did say that "Ace" is coming in from Pittsburgh, and he knows from personal experience that it's really potent. He said that Nick knows it's killing people, but really doesn't give a damn. Nick's only concern is that he can't seem to get enough Ace to supply the demand."

Miller said, "OK. Here's what I'm thinking. We know

that Jensen is involved in heroin distribution and has links to some unknown people in Pittsburgh. Most likely, he contacts them using his cell phone, either texting or calling. Dennis, can we get a search warrant for his phone? I don't want to tip him off, I just want to see if we can connect some of the dots at this point."

Archer thought for a second before responding. "Let's talk about that for a minute. We aren't talking about getting physical access to his phone to see who he's been calling or texting, because that would obviously tip him off. But what we *could* do is get a warrant that authorizes us to track his cell phone location information." Miller looked annoyed and started to say something but Archer continued, "Now before you get all spun up, Chief, how much do you know about cell phone tracking technology?"

"Not much, Dennis. We've never done that, although I understand it's been pretty helpful in some high-profile cases in Pittsburgh. I know that we can get our hands on a record of calls from a specific cell phone, but I'm not sure if that will help us much."

Archer shifted into a professorial mode that reflected an earlier career as a member of the University of Pittsburgh Law School faculty. "OK, first let's talk about how cell phone location information – they call it CSLI – actually works. Most people don't realize it, but as long as your cell phone is turned on it's constantly connecting to nearby cell phone towers, sometimes several times a minute. For each connection, the carrier records the time, the tower location, and the direction and distance from the phone to the tower, and if you a make a phone call they also record the number and the call length.

They keep all of that information for up to five years. If you think about it, since most people keep their cell phone with them everywhere they go, the data can tell us where everyone has been and who they've talked to over the last five years."

Miller nodded, "I can see how that could be pretty helpful. But why do they keep all of that information?"

"Primarily, they do it for business purposes. They use CSLI for billing and to identify weak spots in their networks, things like that. But they also sell aggregated information – with the personal identifiers stripped out – to marketers for several billion dollars each year. The marketers can use that data to figure out things like how many 50-year-old women from wealthy zip codes frequent a given shopping area."

Miller shrugged, "Anything to make a buck, I guess. But it seems to me that the key question for us is how accurate is the individual data?"

"That's a good question, and the answer is that it depends. Sometimes the CSLI data can be nearly as accurate as GPS, other times we can only narrow a location down to a mile or even worse. The biggest factor affecting accuracy is the distance between cell towers in a given area. So, if our guy is in downtown Franklin, we can nail down the location to fifty or a hundred meters. In a more rural area, like between here and Pittsburgh, the towers are spaced pretty far apart and the accuracy will be much lower. The bottom line is that, after we run the CSLI data through a computer program, we can map out where the suspect has been with a pretty high degree of accuracy. Hell, a couple of years ago some politician in Germany got ahold of six months of CSLI for his own phone and it gave a shockingly accurate picture of what he was up to during that period. By looking at the data, you could tell where and when he worked, shopped, went to church, what doctors he saw and the friends he visited."

Chief Miller was excited now. "OK, I'm sold. What do we have to do to get the historical location data for Jensen's phone?"

Archer shrugged and said, "It's a little harder than it used to be, but it shouldn't be any problem. Until recently, I'd just go to a judge and request a 'tracking order' that would authorize the phone company to provide the data. All that I had to show was that the data could provide information 'relevant to an ongoing criminal investigation,' and not even that the specific individual whose information we wanted was a suspect. But, the ACLU and some others went nuts and insisted that law enforcement authorities shouldn't get access to CSLI without satisfying the more stringent requirements for a search warrant. They were concerned that by analyzing historical location data we could get a comprehensive picture of a person's private life. I'll spare you the technical details, but the U.S. Supreme Court agreed with them and held that a warrant is required to access CSLI."

Miller asked, "So, what do we need to do to get a warrant?"

"Before I get to that, I need to tell you that you may run into what we call 'exigent circumstances,' where we can get the information without a warrant. For example, where someone's life is in danger and we don't have time to get a warrant, like a kidnapping. If you run into anything like that, call me. Anyway, getting a warrant for Jensen won't be a problem. I'll need Matt to provide an affidavit demonstrating probable cause that Nick was involved in a criminal activity. Based on what our CI has provided about Nick's involvement in distribution of the Ace of Diamonds, and given how dangerous the drug is, I don't see any trouble getting the warrant. The judge may take a close look at the CI's credibility, but we'll be OK."

Chief Miller said, "You can have Matt whenever you need him. But I have another question. If the cellular carriers are recording all of this information, why can't we get it real-time?"

"We can in some circumstances. Basically, as long as Jensen's phone is turned on, and not in airplane mode, we can track his location. We ask the carrier to ping his phone and give us its location. Heck, they can usually get the phone to report GPS coordinates for a very accurate location – sometimes we can even tell where within a house a suspect is located. The suspect will have no idea that this is happening."

Miller was visibly impressed. "So, can we ask for the real-time data when we go for the warrant?"

Archer said, "That's exactly what we're going to do. Tracking someone real-time is a little more sensitive than getting the historical information, but I don't see any reason why we can't get it given that we have credible information that Jensen is distributing a lethal drug and that he is working with people in Pittsburgh to bring that drug into Franklin."

"Got it. I also heard that there was something called a tower dump?"

"Yeah, we could also ask the phone company to provide a record of all phones that were connected to an individual cell tower during a specific period of time, but that won't do us any good here. That's only useful when we want to establish that someone was in a specific area at a specific time. It can be pretty handy for something like a bank robbery."

Archer looked at a courthouse directory that he kept on his desk and reached for the phone. "Good morning, Judge. Can I get 15 minutes of your time? I need a warrant, and I have the officer with me who can provide the affidavit... Thanks, I'll see you at noon."

Archer turned to Miller, "We're in luck. Judge Crawford will see me at noon, so I need to get to work on drafting an application for the warrant and a supporting affidavit from Matt. I should have a warrant by 12:15. If you can spare Matt for a half-hour I'd like to get going on that right now."

Chief Miller said, "Good plan. Tucker and I will head back to the office while you two get to work. Let me know when you have the warrant."

THREE

Bonesteel's Towing and Auto Body
10 A.M.

Cody looked at his Mustang with decidedly mixed emotions. Franklin was not the kind of town that you could get around in without a car, and there was no question in his mind that he needed wheels to work for Nick. He had used the money that Nick gave him to have Bonesteel's tow his car from the police impound lot and repair the damage caused by MF's shooting spree. He even had enough money left over to replace the rusted-out muffler and the burned out headlight. But, now that he was faced with getting into the car in which Brandi had been murdered, he froze.

Chuck Bonesteel, the owner's son, saw him staring at the Mustang and walked over to see if there was a problem. "Is everything OK, Cody? The car was a bitch to clean up but it looks pretty good to me. We gave it a quick road test and it's running good."

"It's fine, Chuck. You did a great job. I just don't know if I can get in the car after what happened to Brandi."

Bonesteel put his arm around Cody's shoulder. "Take your time, Cody. I can see how that would be hard for you. If you'd like, we can just keep it on the lot until you're ready."

Cody sighed heavily, and didn't respond for a moment as he continued to stare at the car. Finally, he shrugged his shoulders and turned to Bonesteel. "Nah, I'm OK. I just had a flashback to what happened that night, but I'm OK now. I just needed a minute." Cody got in the driver's seat, started the car, and drove off.

Five minutes later, Cody pulled into a deserted parking lot in front of an abandoned gas station and turned off the engine. After making sure that he would not be observed, he reached under the dashboard and probed until he felt a small indentation. He pressed on it, and a hidden panel popped loose, allowing a small plastic bag to fall onto the floor matt. After examining the contents, he muttered, "Dumbshits. Some search. They pulled the car apart and still missed my emergency stash."

Cody tensed as he heard the sound of a car approaching, and then relaxed as the car continued driving on Route 322 towards downtown Franklin. He emptied the plastic bag on the passenger seat, and then carefully examined the small hypodermic needle and the single stamp bag. *If only this had been enough to get us through the night, I wouldn't have gone to that parking lot and Brandi would still be here.* As he thought of Brandi, a tear ran down his face.

He sat quietly for a moment, reflecting on what had happened over the last few weeks. His first reaction was a smug sense of satisfaction at having walked through a minefield and emerging unharmed. That fleeting sense of victory was quickly replaced by an overwhelming sense of panic when he realized that he hadn't really escaped – he was just in a different trap. Sure, he could be a CI and give the cops what they wanted, if Nick didn't kill him first. But, even if he walked, what then? Franklin was a small town and everyone knew his business – the drugs, the series of jobs that he just couldn't hold, the fact that he just didn't get along with most people. Being perfectly honest with himself – a rarity for Cody – he realized that he just didn't have the backbone to pick up and go somewhere new and unfamiliar. At best, his prospects were bleak.

Cody moaned and slowly banged his head on the steering wheel. Why the hell was he going through all of this? He had struggled to get through a cold turkey physical withdrawal from heroin. He had been pretty sick for a couple of days, but he managed. So, now that he was clean, where did that leave him? He had been down that road many times, each time thinking he would quit for good but that never happened.

The thing was, he just looked at things differently now. Everything was just getting to be too much, and he needed a fix to set it right. Yeah, one little fix and everything would be better. He craved the sense of euphoria that would come as soon as he shot up. What was really wrong with that? He could still function well enough to work for Nick until they busted him. Who would know if he pocketed just enough Ace to keep his high? Maybe he could have his cake and eat it too? Yeah, he needed to take the edge off and then he could play out this silly CI game. The cops would get what they wanted, Nick would be out of the picture, and he could walk.

What the hell, Cody thought, *it's not like I can control my fate. The cards have been dealt, and I drew a losing hand. No matter what I do I'm screwed, so why try to fight it? The best I can do is try to dull the pain before I crash and burn. Sure, it would have been nice if I had a passion in life, maybe accomplish something positive. I don't need to change the world, but just for once I'd like to do something that mattered. But, come on, that's just a pipe dream. Where the hell can I do that in Franklin?* The more he thought about it, the more it became clear that the solution was sitting on the seat next to him. Cody's heart beat faster as he picked up the bag and started to prepare his fix.

He hesitated briefly as he realized that he could be heading for an ugly showdown. Matt and the DA had make it clear that all bets were off if they caught him using. *I'll bet they have a pool on how long it takes me to get stoned again. The bastards, they planned this all along – they figured I couldn't stay straight so they'd use me as a CI and still get to throw me off the cliff without going back on their word.* He wasn't sure if Matt was just using him, or whether he really gave a damn. But, for a Marine combat vet Matt had a pretty naïve view of the world. *Screw that self-righteous asshole. He's had all the breaks, let him try walking a mile in my shoes and see how he does.* His mind now made up, Cody took a deep breath and turned back to preparing his fix. Nothing would stop him now.

As he picked up the needle, Cody suddenly had a vision of Brandi sitting beside him in the car. He put the needle down and took a deep breath to calm himself. The apparition was so real that he reached out to touch her, but she vanished. Cody figured that his mind was playing tricks on him. He had tried to convince himself that being in the car where she died wouldn't bother him, but it must be getting to him. Cody reached to pick up the needle but the apparition reappeared and he felt her cold hand on his. She shook her head and mouthed the word "no." And then she was gone.

Jesus Christ, what is going on here? Cody flung open the car door and jumped out. He stood back and stared at the car for a minute, his legs shaking and beads of sweat appearing on his forehead. After calming himself, he slowly approached the car and looked inside, but it was empty. The driver's side door was still open and he reached inside to retrieve his fix and quickly stepped back and slammed the door. After his heartbeat returned to normal he looked around until he found a secluded spot at the back of the abandoned building. Cody checked to be sure that no one could see him, and then examined the needle and heroin bag. *This is for you, Brandi.* Cody paused for a moment, then threw his once precious stash into the woods and walked back to the car. *Yeah, that was for you Brandi.*

FOUR

District Attorney's Office
4 P.M.

Although Dennis Archer expected Chief Miller and Matt Riley to meet him at 4 PM, and knew that they were always punctual, he was on the phone when they appeared at his door. Archer shrugged helplessly and motioned for them to be seated while and he tried to wrap up the call.

Five minutes later, Archer hung up and mimed shattering the phone with a baseball bat. "Sorry about that. I've been stuck on a call with a defense lawyer for half an hour discussing something that should have taken five minutes. Some people just can't take yes for an answer without trying to show you how brilliant they are. I almost pulled a pretty generous plea offer off the table just because he was so obnoxious. But enough of my problems, that's why they pay me the big bucks, right? Did you have any luck with the cell phone data?"

Miller said, "We've made some good progress, Dennis. As soon as Matt got back to the station with the warrant, he downloaded thirty days of location records for Jensen's phone. I have to admit, this high-tech stuff is a little beyond me, but Matt seems to have a flair for it. Anyway, we have a good preliminary analysis but need some more time with the data to really understand it."

Archer said, "Excellent, so what have you turned up?"

Matt jumped into the conversation, "This CSLI tracking is really amazing. It's like being able to rewind someone's life and replay it in front of your eyes. I already have a good feel for how Jensen typically spends his day, and who he hangs out with. It looks like he moved here from Detroit a month or so ago. We're not sure how he ended up here, but the word is that there's some sort of connection between the Detroit and the Pittsburgh gangs. Anyway, he spends a lot of time at a house on Eagle Street, and that seems to confirm what Cody told me about the stash house location. Another thing that could be important is that there is one Pittsburgh number that he either calls or texts twice a week, and a second one that he's only called a couple of times. Those are the only two Pittsburgh numbers that he's used, and since we know the Ace of Diamonds is coming in from Pittsburgh, I'll bet that one or both of them are suppliers."

Archer thought about that for a minute and then said, "Give me the numbers on those phones and I'll see if we can get a warrant for them as well. I think you're right, and this could lead us to the source."

Matt pulled a small notebook from his pocket and wrote the two numbers down on a piece of paper and handed it to Archer.

"OK, I'll need you to do another affidavit. How about the real time data, how are you handling that?"

Miller responded to this question, "It's ready to go, but we haven't started tracking yet since we've been able to keep a pretty good eye on him so far. If he slips us, we'll have the phone company track him. How long did you say the warrant is good for?"

"You've got two weeks."

Miller thought about that for a minute and said, "We better figure it out by then or we'll have a bunch more fatalities. So, what else should we be doing?"

Archer shrugged his shoulders and said, "I think you have the bases covered. Let's talk in the morning and see where we are then."

FIVE

Augustine's Ristorante
4 P.M.

Gus was sitting on a sofa in his office sipping coffee from a china mug and reading the Wall Street Journal when he sensed a presence at his door. Gus didn't bother looking up – Driver was supposed to meet him at 4 PM, there was someone standing silently at his door, and long experience told him that it had to be Driver. Gus was in the middle of an interesting article on the restaurant business, and decided to finish it before he acknowledged his guest.

Driver paused at the door and saw that Gus was occupied, so he walked into the office and sat on a chair facing the sofa. After a minute Gus sensed that Driver was staring at – or perhaps through – the newspaper. Without putting it down, he asked, "Care for some coffee, Driver?"

"No."

Gus finished the article and put the Journal down. He decided to give Driver a taste of his own medicine and stared back at him silently. After a minute of unnerving silence, Gus realized that Driver had no idea that he was being mocked, and would simply wait for Gus to initiate the conversation.

"You said that you had something important to say that

couldn't be discussed on the phone. What is it?"

Driver practically spat the words out with a tone of disgust in his voice, "The Franklin cops have planted a snitch."

That news unsettled Gus. "How did you find this out, Driver?

"The idiot mayor called."

Despite his annoyance over the situation, Gus couldn't help but smile, "I take it that you're referring to His Honor, the beloved Mayor of Franklin, Pennsylvania?"

"Yeah, that asshole. He doesn't know the name of the snitch yet. All he knows is that they call him Agent Blue and he's working with that Franklin cop Matt Riley."

Gus considered that for a moment and said, "We're paying Kelliher a lot of money. Tell him to get the name of this Agent Blue for us or his services will no longer be required."

"I gave him until tomorrow. He said it will be 'difficult.'"

"Difficult? I see. If Kelliher doesn't come up with the name tomorrow perhaps you should encourage him to try a little harder. Perhaps he hasn't been properly motivated."

Driver nodded thoughtfully. "Yeah."

Gus said, "Good. Now, remind me who's running Franklin for us after the recent unpleasantness?"

"Pete Broggi."

Gus had to think for a minute before he could recall Broggi, and then said, "Yes. I was told that he was competent, but I'm beginning to doubt that. We may have to sever our relationship with Mr. Broggi if he doesn't clean up his act. Perhaps you should try to motivate him as well."

"Yes. Anything else?"

"No, Driver. I think that's it."

His business completed, Driver got up and walked out of the office without a further word. Gus shook his head and said to himself, "You're an original Driver. I don't know what I'd do without you." And with that, Gus turned his attention back to the newspaper.

SIX

"Good evening. Welcome to the TV5 News at 10. I'm Bill Masters, and tonight our lead story is once again from Franklin. Mercedes Boone has another of her series of hard-hitting reports of the Western Pennsylvania opioid crisis. Mercedes, can you update us about the situation in Franklin?"

The picture cut from the studio anchor to a close up of the reporter standing in front of the Franklin Police Department. A light snow was falling, as happened many winter days in Franklin, and the reporter's breath was visible as she spoke in the cold night air.

"Yes, Bill. We've had another bizarre turn of events here in Franklin. Earlier this week I reported that the Franklin Police Chief, Robert Miller, had been placed on administrative leave and was the primary suspect in two brutal murders. But, today we learned that Chief Miller has returned to duty and is no longer a suspect. Chief Miller has joined me tonight to explain what has happened."

As Mercedes began her interview the camera zoomed out to include Chief Miller in the picture.

"Chief, I understand that you're back on duty after being on administrative leave for several days. Can you tell us what happened?"

Chief Miller looked directly into the camera and responded in a confident and reassuring manner.

"Sure, Mercedes. As you know, there was a double murder earlier this week, and the evidence initially pointed to me as the primary suspect. Specifically, my pistol and handcuffs were involved. Over the past several days the District Attorney, assisted by the Franklin Police Department and state police, conducted a thorough investigation and concluded that I could not possibly have been at the scene when the murders occurred. So, based on the DA's recommendation, I resumed my duties this morning."

"Chief, can you tell us how the DA determined that you were innocent? And given the fact that the Franklin PD was involved in the investigation, doesn't that undermine the credibility of the determination that you're innocent?"

Ignoring her attempted provocation, Chief Miller responded calmly.

"Those are good questions, Mercedes. While I'm sure that the DA would be happy to explain it in detail to you, the short version is that the coroner's office determined that the murders could only have occurred between 9 PM and midnight on Wednesday. We know that the victims were alive at 9 PM because several witnesses saw them at that time. The coroner determined, based on the temperature and the condition of the bodies, that the time of death was no later than midnight. Numerous witnesses confirmed that I was nowhere near the scene during that period. As to your credibility question, we're talking about science here, not opinion. The coroner used standard, well-tested techniques to determine the time of death with reasonable certainty. Because I was involved in a public event the evening of the murder – now that I think of it, you were there as well – there were numerous witnesses who could testify as to where I was when the murder occurred. So, I think that your concerns about the credibility of our investigation are unfounded."

Mercedes was temporarily flustered by the Chief's mention that she was part of his alibi but quickly gathered her composure and continued,

"Then who was responsible for the murders?"

"We're pursuing a number of leads, Mercedes, but due to the ongoing investigation I can't reveal any of the details of what we've uncovered. I can, however, assure you that we will determine who is responsible for these horrible murders and put them in prison for a long time."

"Do you at least have any motive for the murders, Chief?"

"It's our belief that the murders are drug related. As you know, we've had an opioid problem here in Franklin for several years, and it has escalated to a crisis level over the last several weeks. We suspect that those drugs are coming from Detroit and Pittsburgh, and we're actively investigating the source. I can tell you that stopping the flow of opioids into Franklin, particularly a new variety called 'Ace of Diamonds,' is my highest priority."

"What can you tell us about this 'Ace of Diamonds?' And does that have anything to do with the Officer who was injured a couple of days ago?"

"Concerning your first question, Ace of Diamonds is a mixture of heroin and a far more powerful opioid called fentanyl. It's so powerful that heroin addicts who use Ace of Diamonds and take their usual dose generally OD, sometimes fatally. You've seen the result of that recently here in Franklin, and I don't think we've even seen the worst of it yet. But it wasn't Ace of Diamonds that caused the problem with our Officer – his name is Matt Riley by the way. It appears that he was exposed to an even more powerful drug called carfentanil. We're still investigating what happened."

Although Mercedes smiled sweetly and her voice maintained a pleasant tone, she had been waiting for the right time to spring her next question and hoped that it would cause Miller to lose his composure and give her a good story.

"Chief, some of my sources have suggested that you and the Mayor are engaged in a cover up of the true extent of the Ace of Diamonds crisis. Can you comment on that?"

Miller returned her smile and said,

"Well, I'm glad that you asked that question, Ms. Boone. If there's one thing that I want to accomplish, it's to get the full story out to the public and not to have any kind of cover up. Maybe we can save some lives if people understand just how dangerous this Ace of Diamonds is, and that there are resources available to help addicts. So, I'd like to ask for your help. I've convened an informal group of experts to address the Ace of Diamonds crisis here in Franklin. Since you're so knowledgeable on the topic – you've done a great job with your coverage – I'd like to ask you to join our group. That would give you a chance to see things from the inside and make sure that the public is getting the full story. What do you say?"

Mercedes' smile flickered as she realized that her question had backfired. If she accepted, it would look like she had lost her objectivity. On the other hand, if she rejected the offer she would look like a five-star hypocrite. *I'll be damned, this guy is a lot brighter than I had given him credit for.*

"That's very flattering Chief. Let's talk about it after the broadcast."

"We don't have time to wait, Ms. Boone, people are dying. Let's tell your viewers right now that you're willing to help us save lives. Our first meeting will be at 10 AM tomorrow. Can I count on you joining us?"

Mercedes hesitated as she heard her director yelling in her earpiece to decline, and her usual look of self-confidence dissolved into a momentary look of doubt and confusion. *Sure, if I refuse to help this guy "save lives" I'll come across as a heartless bitch and may as well start looking for a job in a new town.*

"Chief, I'd be happy to help to the extent that my time permits. But as I'm sure you realize, most of my time is devoted to keeping our TV5 viewers informed on all of the important issues that we're facing here in western Pennsylvania. Back to you, Bill."

Once they were off camera, Chief Miller offered his hand and said, "Welcome to our team, Mercedes." As she shook his hand, he continued, "I can tell that you'd really rather be on the outside of the tent pis… ah, throwing the occasional rock, but I really do think that you can help us save some lives. So, I'll promise you this: I may ask that you delay reporting certain facts if we're investigating someone, but you will have complete transparency on what we're doing. You'll get a great story, and together we'll help solve a crisis. Is that acceptable to you?"

Mercedes appeared doubtful, "Chief, I've heard the expression 'outside the tent pissing in rather than inside the tent pissing out' and, believe it or not, that's not what I'm trying to do. And how do I know that you can deliver what you're offering - won't Mayor Kelliher be in charge? Will he agree to this?"

Miller shook his head sadly, "The DA and I have determined that the Mayor's involvement in our opioid task force would be counterproductive. To put a point on it, we don't trust him."

Mercedes was surprised by that comment, and said, "Chief, I know you think that I've tried to set you up, but I'm just doing my job. If I wanted to set you up, I'd quote you on what you just said and let you worry about the consequences. But I'm going to assume that you gave me that information on background. That means I can use the information you gave me, but can't name or quote you directly."

"No, ma'am, I appreciate your candor, but I do know the rules. You can quote me on what I just said. Shall I repeat it so that you can write it down?"

SEVEN

Cody and Josh were sitting at a battered wooden table in the kitchen of a dilapidated duplex. The house, like many of the neighboring properties, was surrounded by a trash-strewn yard that was overgrown with weeds. It couldn't fairly be described as having any particular color because most of the exterior paint had flaked off, although there were random flecks of what might once have been a shade of yellow. Several of the boards on the front porch had rotted away, and the concrete stairs were badly cracked and tilted at an odd angle. On seeing it from the street for the first time, Cody thought that it would make the perfect haunted house for Halloween.

The interior of the house was, if anything, in worse condition than the exterior. The foyer contained remnants of faded wallpaper that had mostly peeled away to reveal cracked and water-stained plaster. Further inside, yellowed linoleum had curled away from the subflooring and portions of the ceiling plaster had collapsed. Trash and pieces of broken furniture were strewn about, and there was a strong, disagreeable odor of sewer gas. Most revolting to Cody, however, was the evidence of rodent infestation throughout the house.

All in all, the house was well suited for its current use as Nick's stash house. This was not a house that would be visited by anyone not having business there. The only thing that could be said to be in good condition was a large safe concealed in the closet of a back bedroom. Tonight, the safe contained several loaded 9 mm pistols, several hundred rounds of ammunition, a package containing a kilo of Ace of Diamonds, numerous bags of Ace, a lesser quantity of cocaine and $185,000 in cash. Such were the tools of Nick's trade.

"You seem to be getting the hang of things pretty quickly," Josh said.

"Enough to know that we're short of Ace, and no way are we going to make it through next week."

"No sweat, Cody, two more keys are coming in tonight. I'm just waiting for a text telling us where we'll meet up. Eduardo will do the actual pickup for us, but we don't know who the courier from Pittsburgh will be."

"So, how's that work?"

"None of your fucking business, man. The way it works is only Eduardo and I get the details, and you just stick to the housekeeping stuff. I'll let you know when the delivery gets here, and you just worry about getting it packaged and into distribution. Watch your mouth, though, Nick hears you asking about shit like that and he'll burn your ass for sure."

"Hey, I'm not trying to learn any of your goddamned state secrets. I just want to be sure we're going to have enough Ace to do some business. No big deal."

"Yeah, well, just don't worry about the supply end of the business. We've got some interesting people in Franklin on the payroll, so things go pretty smoothly." Josh suddenly wore a frightened look. "Cody, ah, you didn't hear that. No kidding, you breathe a word of that to Nick and we're both dead. Got it?"

Cody said, "Hear what?"

"Ok, good. You're learning. I need to take a quick piss, and then we're outta here."

Josh set his phone on the table and headed for the bathroom. A minute later, Cody heard the sound of an incoming text from Josh's phone and saw the screen light up. Glancing up quickly to make sure that Josh was not returning, Cody spun the phone towards him and read the text:

Sun, 6 PM, 9th & Buffalo, brown Corolla w/racing stripe

The screen blacked out before Cody could read the rest of the message, and he quickly slid it back to its original spot on the table just before Josh returned.

Josh picked up the phone and noticed that a new text had arrived. He looked at the text, grunted, and turned to Cody, "Let's go."

EIGHT

Matt's Cabin
5 P.M.

Matt was enjoying a day off. He was standing behind the cabin checking on a roast that was slow-cooking in his smoker while Erin was preparing some appetizers in the kitchen. The only glitch in what has been an otherwise fabulous day was the glass of wine that he held in his hand. Erin had proudly brought a bottle with her that she said would go great with the roast. A "Côte Rôtie" she called it, something that the guy in the wine store said came from France's Rhône Valley and was supposed to be one of the 'finest, most sensual' wines. *How the hell can a wine be sensual? As much as he wanted to please Erin by enjoying the wine, it tasted and smelled like vomit. Then, a simple solution occurred to him. Matt glanced furtively behind him and, when he saw the coast was clear, poured all but a small sip on the ground. Now all I have to do is ask for a refill before I come back to check on the roast. Then maybe I can get a damned beer.*

Feeling satisfied that he had dodged that particular bullet, Matt started to walk into the house to check on Erin when his cell phone rang. He saw that the caller was Cody and decided that he better take the call. "Hey, Cody. Glad you called

How would you like the rest of a bottle of fine French wine?"

"What the hell are you talking about?"

"I'm just kidding. Erin bought some fancy French wine that tastes like something crawled into the bottle and died. But I've solved that problem. So, what's up?"

Cody's tone was serious. "Matt, I just found out a couple of things that you need to hear. First, there's two kilos of Ace coming into Franklin from Pittsburgh tomorrow night at six. They're bringing it into town in a brown Corolla with a racing stripe on it, and the drop off point is 9th and Buffalo."

Matt was suspicious. "How the hell did you find that out?"

"I lucked out. They didn't tell me. Josh went to the bathroom and left his phone sitting on the table with me and a text came in with the details. They don't know that I know."

"OK, that's one shipment that isn't going to make it onto the street. Since they don't know that you know about it, they won't have any reason to think that you ratted them out. What else do you have?"

Cody said, "I don't really know what to make of this, but Josh told me that they have someone 'very interesting' on the payroll here in Franklin making sure that no one hassles them. He didn't tell me who it was, and after it slipped out he freaked out and told me that if I told anyone we'd both be dead. That's all I got."

"Any ideas who it might be?"

After a brief pause, Cody said, "Matt, I haven't a fucking clue. But be careful because Josh could trace that back to me if it gets out."

"No sweat. I'll hold that real close and just use it to try to put the pieces of the puzzle together. You done good, Cody.

Keep it up. Anything else we need to talk about?"

"Nah, that's it for now."

"OK, check in with me again tomorrow at the usual time." With that, Matt ended the call.

NINE

Nick was not a morning person. Last night, like most nights, he had rolled into bed around 4 AM in a drunken haze. It was not as if Franklin had a vibrant nightlife – in fact, it had none at all – but Nick believed that didn't mean a man couldn't party. But, for him, parties had their limits. Despite his business – or perhaps because of it – he avoided hard drugs. So this morning, like most mornings, his head throbbed and his stomach rebelled at the thought of food. He vowed that he'd never drink that much again.

Thirty minutes earlier, he had been jarred awake by the sound of incoming texts on the cell phone that he had left on his nightstand. After achieving a grumpy level of awareness, Nick quickly scanned the texts and saw nothing of consequence. He showered, and then decided to go to the Epoch Coffee House for a light breakfast. There, he ordered a latte and a plain bagel, and found a comfortable corner table at the back of the shop, far away from other people and their irritating noises.

Nick had barely had time to sit down and take the first sip of his latte when the sound of another incoming text jarred his brain. Bleary eyed, he squinted at the message:

> **"Meet me at Grove City Brew Pub, 2 PM. Important. Pete."**

Who the fuck does this guy think he is? He can kiss my ass. Nick responded:

> **"Can't make it – why don't you come here around 5?"**

What is so damned important that we have to meet this afternoon? The Ace is coming in as scheduled, and I don't know of any problems.

The text sounded again.

> **"NO. MEET ME AT 2 PM OR WE SHUT IT DOWN."**

Crap, I can't let that happen. Once I have everything running smoothly I'll find another supplier. I don't need this shit.

After a slight pause Nick responded:

> **"Fine. See u there."**

Nick saw that he had plenty of time, and then turned back to his breakfast. His hope for a quiet, uninterrupted breakfast evaporated a few minutes later when Josh appeared at his table.

"Grab a seat," Nick mumbled through a mouthful of bagel. "What the hell do you want?"

"I just stopped in for a cup of coffee and saw a walking

cadaver that looked a lot like you sitting here," Josh said with a conspiratorial smile.

"Yeah, last night was pretty intense. Tell me something, Josh, is there something going on that I need to know about? I just got a text from our Pittsburgh contact *ordering* me to meet him at 2 in Grove City. Who the *hell* does he think he is *ordering* me to do anything? Anyway, the prick told me that he'd shut us down if I didn't show up."

Josh thought for a moment and then said, "I haven't a clue, Nick. Everything seems to be cool."

"Well, something's up, that for sure, and I don't think he wants to meet to give me a gold star for good customer service. Find Eduardo and tell him where I'm going. I'll need him to be in the restaurant an hour before my meeting to make sure that I'm not being set up. Tell him to act like he doesn't know me, but be ready to nail Pete if he threatens me. Get going, and call me if there are any problems."

Josh stood up and before heading out the door said, "Got it. He'll be there."

TURNING THE TABLES

ONE

Benjamin's Roadhouse

Noon

Dennis Archer was already seated when Chief Miller walked into Benjamin's. It was their custom to meet here once a week, in part because over the years they had become close friends and genuinely enjoyed each other's company, in part because it was an efficient way to do business. The hostess, knowing that they preferred some degree of privacy, sat them away from other tables. While it was understood between them that some things could not be discussed over lunch, they typically were able to cover quite a bit of ground in an hour.

"Afternoon, Dennis," Chief Miller said as he hung his coat over the back of the chair and sat down. "That hot coffee looks pretty good to me. I know what I'm having, are you ready to order?"

"Sure." Archer beckoned the waitress, and she came to the table. "Coffee for the Chief, I'll have the spinach salad. Chief?"

"I'll have the Ben Franklin burger. None of that rabbit food for me."

The waitress scribbled their orders on her pad and headed

for the kitchen. As soon as she left, Archer said, "OK, let's get down to it. I was able to get a warrant on the two Pittsburgh cell phone numbers that Jensen has been calling. The judge thought our probable cause demonstration was a bit thin, but given the Ace of Diamonds crisis he was in an unusually receptive mood."

Miller interjected, "Yeah, Matt updated me this morning."

"Have you turned up anything new?"

Miller paused for a second to organize his thoughts. "Yeah. The number that Nick calls regularly belongs to a guy in Pittsburgh named Peter Broggi. The interesting thing is that it looks like they've met once in person – at least they were in the same place, and I don't think it was a coincidence – up at the airport. We know that Broggi came in on the commuter plane just before the meeting because he never turned his phone off and, although the coverage drops out pretty often during the flight, we could track him all the way from Pittsburgh."

Archer said, "Well, I guess that's something. What about the other number?"

They both paused silently as the waitress came back with their food. After she served them, Miller leaned in close to Archer and quietly said, "That's an odd one. It belongs to a guy named Nicolae Ceausescu. We ran him, and he shows up clean as a whistle. The phone doesn't get used very much. But here's the thing – the data shows that he's had a few calls with Mayor Kelliher. The latest call was Thursday morning at 8:35 – it looks like as soon as we ended the meeting the Mayor called this guy, and they talked for two minutes."

Archer dropped a fork full of salad into his plate and

stared incredulously at Miller. "I wonder what the hell that was about?"

Miller locked eyes with Archer, "It gets even worse."

"Dennis, Agent Blue heard that the Pittsburgh gang is paying someone in Franklin a lot of money to make sure that they don't have any problems bringing drugs into town. No names, just the fact that someone 'interesting' is being paid."

"You thinking what I'm thinking?"

Miller had a disgusted look on his face as he said, "Yeah, I think our esteemed Mayor may be on the take. I have some ideas on how we can nail his ass."

Archer nodded and said, "Good. Let's do this right. I want an airtight case – no evidentiary problems or procedural screw-ups that a defense attorney can use – so that we can put the bastard away for a long time. How about the real-time data, any luck with that?"

"Yeah, we're using it to keep an eye on Nick Jensen. Looks like he slept in this morning, and last I heard he was across the street at Epoch. If that's their type of clientele, I think I'll have to find a new coffee shop."

Archer said, "Well, I'm glad that it's working, but I can't say that where Jensen is having breakfast is exactly front page news."

"Let's just see where this leads us. I have a hunch that Jensen is going to lead us to some bigger fish."

With the morning's business out of the way, Miller and Archer moved on to a discussion of why the Pittsburgh Penguins were in a slump. Archer, who had roots in Boston and remained a Bruins fan, couldn't resist needling the Chief. "The problem is that expansionist teams like the Penguins just haven't got the hang of hockey yet, they just get lucky every once in a while. The NHL has gone downhill ever since they expanded from the Original Six."

Miller smiled insincerely and said, "Kiss my ass, Dennis."

TWO

Nick was in a foul mood when he walked into the pub. He looked around and noticed Pete sitting at a table in the corner of the restaurant with a mug of beer on the table. After scanning the rest of the room, and noticing that Eduardo was sitting at the end of the bar out of Pete's line of vision, Nick walked over to Pete's table and sat down. "Pete, what the hell is so important that I have to drive down here on a couple of hours' notice? I've got better things to do than keep you entertained. If you need a friend, go buy a fucking dog."

Pete stared at Nick for a moment. *I'm glad we didn't do this over lunch. This guy, with his foul mouth and scuzzy appearance, turns my stomach.* "You tell me if it was worth the drive. You have a snitch working for you. I didn't want to discuss it with you on the phone or by text and take the chance that someone else might find out that we know. We needed to have our little talk today to minimize the damage that *your* carelessness has caused."

Nick was both stunned at the news and annoyed at Pete's condescending attitude, and he snarled back at Pete. "I'm gonna give you the benefit of a large doubt that you know

what you're talking about. Who's the goddamned snitch? The fucker won't live to see the sunrise tomorrow morning."

"We don't know. All that we know so far is that the cops have someone inside your organization who they call Agent Blue, and he tipped them about the MF murder. We're working on the name, but we do know that the Franklin cop who used to be in the Marines, Matt Riley, is handling the snitch."

"I know who you mean. He's been a flaming pain in the ass for us, busted several of my guys and just isn't getting the word to back off. I thought you guys had things greased with the cops? Doesn't matter, Riley dies this afternoon."

Pete locked eyes with Nick and there was steel in his voice. "Listen to me very, very carefully Nick. *We* will deal with Officer Riley in a way that I'm sure you will find satisfactory. *You* will do nothing. This has to be handled right or it'll bring a world of hurt down on us. If you make a move on Riley, some very important people will be highly pissed, if you take my meaning."

Nick bristled at the fact that he wouldn't be allowed to fix a problem that was affecting his own gang. He noticed that Eduardo had picked up on the increasing level of hostility, and had slipped his hand into his jacket where it no doubt gripped a pistol. Eduardo slowly rotated his bar stool so that it appeared that he was checking out a different game on a TV to his left, but in reality he was preparing to react quickly if necessary. Nick met Eduardo's eyes briefly and gave him a subtle signal to do nothing. "Fine. But let me know what happens."

"Sure. I thought about not telling you and just taking care of the problem, but I think you need to know about this. It's in both of our interests for you to keep your eyes open for any

signs of who the snitch might be." Since Nick had not pushed back on dealing with Matt Riley, Pete decided to throw in a peace offering. "If we find out who this Agent Blue is, he's all yours to deal with any way you'd like."

Nick grinned at that. "Deal. You got anything else or can I get back to business?"

Pete shook his head, "Nah, isn't that enough for one day?" Pete and Nick got up from the table and walked together to the parking lot. When they reached the sidewalk, Pete turned to Nick and said, "I'll be in touch as soon as we turn something up on the snitch. And believe me, we'll get a name." Pete ignored Nick's outstretched hand and then walked to his car.

◆

Lieutenant Ray Tucker was sitting in an unmarked car a discrete distance away from, but with a clear view of, the entrance to the Grove City Brew Pub. Under different circumstances Tucker would have been happy to wander in and grab a cold one, some pub grub and maybe check out some of the local girls. But this afternoon he had a job to do.

Tucker was amused by the fact that he was here at this place and time because of an unintended consequence of modern technology. Most people embraced the convenience of having GPS-based navigation apps on their cell phones, but ignored the fact that it was a two-way street: the same technology that told them where they were and how to get somewhere else could also surreptitiously reveal their location to others. Today, Nick's iPhone provided a beacon that allowed Tucker to follow him, and thereby begin to understand the Ace of Diamonds pipeline.

This morning, a ping of Nick's phone revealed that he was at the Epoch Coffee Shop. Tucker parked a block away and watched until Nick got into his car and drove west on Liberty Street. Tucker discretely trailed Nick as he turned onto 15th Street and then south on Route 8. After that, Tucker rarely had Nick in sight, but periodic GPS pings guided him as he followed Nick onto Route 80 and then Route 79 towards Pittsburgh. After forty-five minutes, Tucker had begun to wonder if he was on a wild goose chase when Nick turned into a mall parking lot and parked in front of the Grove City Brew Pub.

Tucker parked nearby and sat in his car for ten minutes before getting out to stretch his legs. He worried that Nick might elude him by slipping out the back door. But, since he was here by himself and out of his jurisdiction, there wasn't a damned thing he could do about it. Tucker returned to his car and after another fifteen minutes Nick emerged with a man who he mentally cataloged as suspect, white male, approximately five-foot-nine-inches, medium build and black hair. Tucker didn't notice the small Hispanic man who left the pub about 30 seconds later.

Nick and his companion had a brief conversation. Tucker thought it odd that the companion refused to shake hands when they parted. The unidentified man headed to a red 2017 Corvette Z06 convertible that was parked three cars away. Tucker casually got out of his car and walked past the suspect, pretending to admire the car but in reality noting that it had a Pennsylvania vanity license plate "PB Vette." *That red Corvette sure must attract attention. It looks like it's speeding when it's parked.*

While Tucker radioed Matt and asked him to run the license plate, the sound of squealing tires and the throaty roar of a powerful V-8 engine announced the Corvette's departure from the parking lot. That was followed by the sound of a siren, and Tucker burst into laughter when he saw that a local cop had observed the Corvette's spectacular exit from the parking lot and pulled it over. *Serves you right, dumbass. Now let's see what we can find out about you.*

Matt radioed back in a couple of minutes. "The car is registered to a Peter R. Broggi of Pittsburgh. No outstanding warrants, but I think we just connected some of the dots. The phone number that Nick Jensen has been calling regularly is also registered to a Peter Broggi of the same address."

Tucker replied, "Yeah, and this is no low-level courier. He's driving a Corvette Z06 that must have set him back close to a hundred grand."

THREE

Epoch Coffee House
3 P.M.

Nick had been parked for fifteen minutes in the lot behind Epoch and was getting impatient. He relaxed a bit when Eduardo parked next to him and got out of his car. As Eduardo climbed into the passenger seat of the Escalade, Nick snarled, "Where the fuck have you been?"

Eduardo ignored the question and said, "You sure took a lot of shit from Pete. I thought I was going to have to pop him until you signaled me to back off. What the hell was that all about?"

Nick said, "I wasn't sure how that was going to come down, but you were positioned perfectly. The clueless asshole never knew that you were sitting behind him. It's just a matter of time until he cops that attitude with someone and gets blown away."

After a quick sip of his coffee Nick continued, "Anyway, Pete says that the cops have a snitch working for us. We need to figure who it is, and when we do, I'm going to have a little job for you."

Eduardo nodded and then said, "Boss, you've got another big problem. Someone followed you to Grove City."

"No fucking way. You know I'm careful about that, and nobody was on my tail."

"Maybe, but there was someone in a black Taurus with a police interceptor package parked about three cars away from Pete. Unmarked, but it was pretty obvious. When Pete got in his Vette the guy got out of his car and pretended that he was just casually walking by. As soon as Pete pulled out, he went back to his car and got on his radio. You can bet that he has ID'd Pete by now." Eduardo passed his phone over to Nick and said, "I got a picture of him. The reason I'm late is that I followed the dude back to Franklin. And, no shit, when he got here he pulled into the police department parking lot. So, don't give me any crap about not being followed."

Nick pounded his steering wheel. "What the hell is going on? I know that he wasn't tailing me. Most of the time there wasn't anyone in sight on the highway, so maybe it's just a coincidence?"

"No way. He perked up when you came out, and really tuned in when you and Pete were talking in the parking lot. That ain't no friggin coincidence, he was waiting for you."

Nick had a sinking feeling in the pit of his stomach as it dawned on him that Eduardo was right. "Call Josh and tell him to get his ass over here right now. Tell him I want him to steer clear of Eagle Street, and not to tell anyone what he's doing."

By coincidence, Josh had just walked into the Epoch when his phone rang. When he saw that it was Eduardo, whom he thought of as a pompous little prick, he briefly debated not answering. Then again, Eduardo rarely called, and when he did he was almost always calling for Nick. "Hola, Eduardo.

Qué pasa?" Josh listened for a minute and then said, "No problem, I'm at Epoch now." He hung up the phone just as the barista put his coffee on the bar, then turned and walked out the back door.

FOUR

Mayor's Office
4 P.M.

Walter Kelliher pulled into his reserved parking space at City Hall and reached for his brief case. He had avoided stopping by the office all day, but had to finish some year-end paperwork. He figured that should only take a half hour or so, and after a quick drink he would head home and take Margaret out to dinner. She had been uncommonly nice to him lately, and it was the least he could do.

As he walked down the corridor he noticed that the light was on in his office. *That's odd, I'm sure that I turned the lights off when I left yesterday.* Kelliher unlocked his office door, and when he stepped into the room the high-back chair behind his desk swiveled to face him, revealing a well-dressed, muscular man with a large scar on the left side of his face. The man pointed to a chair and commanded, "Close the door and sit."

Kelliher quietly sat in the chair and faced Driver, the man who delivered his monthly payoff, but whose presence tonight was ominous. Driver snarled, "Give me the name of Agent Blue." Kelliher froze and, instead of one of his usual glib responses, all that issued from his fear-constricted throat was an indecipherable, raspy grunt.

Driver obtained a near erotic pleasure from watching Kelliher panic and thought, *let's see if I can make him piss his pants* He stared threateningly at Kelliher for a moment, and then pulled a switchblade knife from his pocket and casually released the blade with a chilling metallic click. He idly inspected the blade and then used the tip to remove a stray piece of dirt from beneath one of his fingernails. Driver then returned his attention to Kelliher and calmly announced, "I think you will die very slowly, and very, very painfully. Stand up."

Visibly shaking, Kelliher slowly stood up. Driver stared at him silently for a full minute, watching the sweat bead on Kelliher's face and soak the armpits of his shirt, before Kelliher sobbed, "Please, I can get the name. Just give me 24 hours I promise."

Driver snarled, "Bullshit. You think this is some kind of game? Put your hands on the desk."

With tears now streaming down his face, Kelliher complied. "Please, you don't need to do this. I'll get the name for you."

Driver continued to stare coldly, and then held the blade in front of Kelliher's face. "I said put your hands on the desk." Kelliher, his eyes wide with fear, slowly placed his badly shaking hands on the table. "Are you left handed or right handed?"

Kelliher gasped, and in a barely audible voice said "Right."

"Then you better learn to do things left-handed." Still staring directly into Kelliher's eyes, Driver raised the knife above his head and then slammed it toward Kelliher's right hand. The blade sunk deeply into the desk's wooden surface with a solid thud, just to the left of where the hand had been

Kelliher had passed out in fear before the knife had struck, and lay on the floor with a spreading circle of wetness in his crotch. Driver laughed contemptuously. *Just as I thought, he pissed himself.*

Driver splashed some water onto Kelliher's face. The Mayor slowly regained consciousness and, as his mind focused, squeamishly checked his right hand. Seeing that he was unhurt, he sighed with relief. Driver snickered, and then ordered in a harsh voice, "Stand up."

Kelliher slowly struggled to his feet and steadied himself on a chair. "Last chance. Get me the name by tomorrow." Driver turned and walked out the door.

FIVE

Route 8, Franklin
6 P.M.

Matt Riley had been sitting in an unmarked Taurus for more than a half hour, and was beginning to think that he was wasting his time. He was parked along Route 8, just across from the Venango County Regional Airport, in a location that allowed him to observe traffic coming into Franklin from Pittsburgh. Based on Cody's tip, he was looking for a brown Corolla. There was an officer discretely observing the drop off point, but Matt was monitoring traffic coming into Franklin in case that had been changed.

Matt decided that he'd wait another 15 minutes and then call it a night. Several cars sped past him at well above the posted speed limit, but unless someone did something really dumb - or happened to be driving a brown Corolla - they would get a pass from this particular unmarked cop car. Five minutes later, as Matt was pouring a mug of coffee from his thermos, he spotted a five-year-old brown Toyota Corolla driven by a young male heading towards Franklin. The car was obeying the speed limit, and not acting in any way suspiciously.

Matt pulled onto Route 8 and followed the Toyota at a

decent interval as it headed towards downtown Franklin, carefully observing the vehicle for any traffic violations. He called in the license plate number, but there were no outstanding violations or warrants. After about a mile, the Toyota changed lanes abruptly to pass another vehicle. Matt thought about making a stop on the pretext of an illegal lane change, but decided to follow the car for a bit longer. After another mile, the Toyota signaled and made a right hand turn onto Eagle Street.

Eddy Martinez was no fool. He had been making the run from Pittsburgh to Franklin for two years and had never been caught. As he passed the airport, he noticed an unmarked police car. *Seriously, who the hell do you think you're fooling?* He didn't worry when he saw the cop pull onto the highway, but carefully kept his speed just below the limit and did nothing that would give the cop a reason to stop him. His eyes lingered on his rear-view mirror a little too long, and when he looked forward again, he was startled by a slow-moving car with its lights turned off. His tires screeched as he swerved hard left and narrowly missed the darkened car. *Shit. Not too smooth, man. Well, if the cop wanted to stop me, that sure as hell was his excuse.*

A cautious man by nature, Martinez signaled and turned right onto Eagle Street to see if the cop would follow. He started to worry when the cop followed him. Martinez turned onto 12th Street and continued until he had to stop at the light on Liberty Street; the unmarked car was right behind him but made no move to pull him over. He began to sweat and felt his pulse quicken. *Goddamn it, if they catch me with what I'm carrying tonight I'll spend at least twenty years in prison. Just*

be calm, the cop doesn't have any reason to stop me.

When the light turned green, Martinez signaled and turned left onto Liberty Street. He found a parking place across the street from Benjamin's Roadhouse, a restaurant that he'd been to a few times before and really liked. *Let's see what the cop does now.*

It was decision time for Matt: pull in behind the Toyota or go around the block. On impulse, Matt parked behind the Toyota, turned off his headlights and waited to see what happened. For two minutes both drivers sat in their cars, pretending to be unaware of each other.

As Martinez watched the unmarked car behind him his heart began to race. *Oh, SHIT. Man, what's going on here? Just be cool, take the ticket and act like it's no big deal. He's got no right to search the car.* But nothing happened, the cop just sat there pretending that he was checking his phone. *What the fuck is he doing just sitting there? Just get out of the car and walk over to the restaurant and see what happens.* Martinez was frozen in indecision, and finally the tension got to him. As if it had a mind of its own, his hand shifted the car into drive and he floored the accelerator. As the Toyota fishtailed out of the parking place, Matt flipped on the flashing lights concealed in the car's grill and raced after the Toyota. Matt radioed in, "*Unit 7 in pursuit of a brown, late model Toyota Corolla heading north on Liberty Street. I need backup.*"

Martinez raced up Liberty Street and took the sharp turn onto Route 8 heading back towards the airport. Matt's car shadowed him, its flashing lights filling Martinez's rear view mirror. Another police car was a quarter mile ahead and closing the distance between them rapidly. Martinez, realizing

that he was trapped, slammed on the brakes and leapt from the Toyota before it had stopped. He hit the pavement hard and rolled, then sprinted in front of an oncoming 18-wheeler. The truck's air horn blasted and its tires screeched as Martinez vanished into the darkness.

Matt's car slid to a stop behind the Toyota, and he cringed as he watched Martinez narrowly dodge the huge truck. The truck's brakes locked up, and it jackknifed across the road. Matt radioed his backup to secure the Toyota and took off on foot after Martinez down Eagle Street. The chase was over before it started. Martinez had vanished into the shadows of Eagle Street. Matt walked back across Route 8 and joined a group of his colleagues at the brown Toyota.

SIX

Pittsburgh
Sunday, December 31
2 P.M.

Matt had planned a special New Year's Eve surprise for Erin, and the suspense was building. He told her that they would be gone overnight and that she should bring a nice dress suitable for an "elegant venue," but refused to provide any further details. The plan was to leave Matt's cabin at 2 PM and drive to their destination. By the time that Matt pulled onto Route 79 South, Erin was confident that they would spend the evening in Pittsburgh. What they would do there, however, remained a mystery.

After an hour and a half drive to Pittsburgh, they began weaving their way through congested downtown streets, many of which were barricaded for the First Night celebration. They finally arrived at the William Penn Hotel, a majestic building dating from 1916, and Matt turned their luggage over to the bellman. Erin was excited, but as they entered the lobby she feigned a stern tone and said, "This is a beautiful hotel, Matt, but enough of the mystery. Where are we going tonight?"

"What makes you so sure we're doing anything other than checking into a hotel for a romantic evening?"